MW01223689

This novel's story and characters are fictitious. Certain long-standing institutions, agencies, and public offices are mentioned, but the characters involved are wholly imaginary.

First Edition

Catch the Adventure:

www.sean-oneil-writer.com

The Omega Variant

Preface

Sometimes we find ourselves living in challenging times. That would certainly be the opinion of those who lived through events such as WWI, the Spanish flu, and WWII.

It also became the belief of those who lived through the Covid-19 pandemic. Eighty years of relative stability had lowered the bar on facing a crisis. People equated wearing a mask and staying at home with storming the beaches of Normandy. Rights triumphed over responsibilities. Stupidity and conspiracies reigned in a time where sensibility was sorely needed. It was all driven by small-minded people desperate to exert influence and control.

Ultimately, the pandemic passed, for the most part, that was. The world found a cure. Science found a cure. It was in the form of a vaccine. A simple needle in the arm and the world could do what was impossible to do in 1918.

However, as simple as it seemed on the surface, the world had become a much more complicated place than it was back in 1918. Social platforms allowed for opinions and false narratives to find homes. News had become media, slanted to the left and right based on the mindset of the owners. So, what should have been simple, wasn't. What would have seemed like a gift from heaven for those who had lived through the Spanish flu was met with a degree of skepticism, and worse.

In the end, the event split the world between those who followed science and those who followed conspiracy. More specifically, those who sought medical immunity, and those who did not.

The Omega Variant

A World in Chaos

One day, life as normal stopped. It wasn't due to war, an asteroid strike, or zombies. It was from the tiniest of threats. A microbe, one that was invisible to the naked eye, swept out of Wuhan, China in December 2019.

Within just a few months, what seemed to be a world away was suddenly on everyone's front steps. Europe was in chaos; people were dying in the streets of Italy. Spain ran out of places to store the dead bodies. Once the virus reached America, the shit then hit the fan.

With the failure of the WHO, each country was on its own. Policy depended on the slant of the government. China, with its autocratic structure, quickly locked down and contained the spread. Western countries struggled to try to find the balance between the economy and health. The more right-wing the government, the more deaths it took before containment measures were put in place.

History, conveniently, had provided the world with a blueprint for such an event. The 1918 Spanish flu was a perfect model. The multiple waves model of 1918 was mimicked by Covid in 2020. While the 1918 model should have been a guide to the world, no one wanted to hear it. The world, in 2020, had become used to quick and easy. Eighteen months or more and multiple waves were simply not acceptable.

In America, the right-wing Trump administration created enough disinformation that pockets of disbelievers eventually turned into groups hell-bent against vaccines and masks. As is often the case, what is made in America is exported to the rest of the world. Other right-wing governments followed similar approaches.

In the end, by late 2022, the pandemic had finally simmered down. By that point, some 60% of the world was fully inoculated which was almost enough for herd immunity but not quite. The bigger problem was the lack of uniformity. Some countries, such as Canada, hit 94%, while poorer countries in Africa and Asia struggled to reach 40%.

In America, while the country as a whole was over 70%, the coverage region to region was very patchy. The challenge for the government was what to do about it. Immunity passports provided a level of control but there were increasingly violent actions by the 30% who felt their rights were being impeached.

Once things had settled down, America decided on a color-coded county rating system based on a series of metrics. The leading metrics were vaccines percentage and case levels. Based on the metrics, counties were assigned a green, yellow or red code.

Red counties and regions of red countries were secured from the outside by the military checkpoints that managed transportation in and out. In these regions, those with immunity passports moved freely in and out, while those without did not, under any circumstances. The idea was it would drive vaccination rates up in those target regions.

Without an immunity passport in a yellow zone, individuals needed to accept an instant Covid test to travel to a green zone.

The system worked reasonably until the spring of 2023 when Donald Trump ran for the presidency once again. He and his team ran based on conspiracy theories including questioning the vaccine and the reality of Covid.

While he lost again, the world slipped a little backward. That was bad news as 2025 was to see the worst variant yet, the Omega variant.

In the end, the world did find out the virus was man-made, in a lab in Wuhan, China. The Chinese never meant to inflict it upon the world. It was an accident. It was the kind of accident that happens when people fiddle with things they should not. Ultimately, they had opened Pandora's box and couldn't close it again.

Over time, variants had become the norm, so when Omega came along, no one batted an eye. It was just another one in an ongoing cycle, or so it seemed.

The funny thing was, even if the full Omega variant news had been available on day one, most people would not have believed it or cared. Truth, in the world, had died.

It was when the Omega variant made its way to America that the true apocalypse began.

Revisiting Past

In November 2024, with the Republicans winning Congress back, the government immediately lightened the restriction on red and yellow zones. They also removed the incentives for further vaccinations. The result was a slow, but steady increase in Covid cases and, once again, deaths.

By summer 2025, cases and deaths were back near 2020 levels. The difference, in this case, was that the cases and deaths were highly concentrated in the red zones. However, even the deaths in those zones did little to change the prevailing mindset of rights over responsibility. People felt they had survived the virus, and it was time to move one, despite the fact that it continued to morph.

There were four major regions of concern in America, each encompassing multiple counties. In some cases, these regions contained hundreds of counties crossing state lines. The areas included a large portion central to northern Texas, northern Colorado through Wyoming, the Bible Belt, and Florida up into Georgia. The areas had become flashpoints for new variants.

A steep increase in cases through the summer of 2024 had brought back containment methods, despite Republican wishes. It further isolated the red zones which only hardened the resolve of many within them not to give in to the system.

Messaging from the administration did little to change vaccination rates. It was hard for those in the government to step back from their support of crazy theories, the ones that had helped them get elected. It wasn't about being sensible anymore. Conspiracy theories had become part of daily life.

What evolved over that period was growing animosity between the green and the red zones. By the time fall 2025 rolled around, and Omega really kicked in, the country was prime for a civil war.

Lafayette, Alabama

Lilly had always loved her town. She had been born and raised in Lafayette. It was all she knew, but that didn't matter, for her, it was all she needed.

She married in Lafayette and had always believed she would die there too. What she hadn't expected was that she would die so young.

She was only thirty-two but she had Covid, the latest variant. They said it came in from Africa, via the Caribbean, the same way the slaves had so many years before. The truth was, no one was sure. It didn't matter to Lilly where it came from. The fact was it had taken ahold of her and was doing what it did best, reproducing en masse inside her.

She was a Republican by affiliation although she had never been a political person. She was Republican because her family was Republican. The family was devoted followers of Trump and QAnon. She had never had any issues with the vaccine but was told by both her family and her husband that there was no way she was going to get one.

So, as she lay on a hospital bed on a ventilator, alone in the ICU, she wondered where her God was and whether or not she had made the best decisions in life. The window on decisions had passed. Where her God was, she would find out soon enough as the virus ravaged the last of her life away.

Liberty, Texas

Will sat in Jack's Bar and Grill watching Fox News. The broadcast was covering the latest news on the new Covid variant. It mentioned the likelihood of further lockdowns and vaccine requirements.

"Y'all see that damn news. They saying we gonna be locked down in this region until we take that fucken vaccine," Will said as he held court at the end of the bar.

"Well, I ain't never taking it. We wouldn't have this shit if Trump were still president," an older man from across the bar replied.

"Damn right," Will replied picking away at the label on his Bud Light.

Will looked around the bar. It was his home away from home. More accurately, it was his home, all that was missing was a bed. It was more a bar than a grill. There was a little grill in the back that pushed out enough simple items to keep the regulars on their stools.

He took out a cigarette and lit it up. The smoke only added to the haze in the old place. The bar had sat on that corner of the old interstate for as long as he could remember. He had his first beer there and his first fight.

"Yo, Will, what we gonna do about the blockades? Them Greens are trying to shut us all down," a voice from a back table asked.

Will knew who asked. He knew the voice. He knew every voice in the bar. It was the regular afternoon crowd, his crowd.

"Fuck 'em, Johnny. They think we care about leaving. We don't, we're good here. I know I'm good here. What do y'all need with somewhere else?"

Across the bar, the dozen or so men all nodded. They all quietly agreed that life was just fine in their corner of red zone Liberty.

"Yo, Jack, grab me another Bud Light," Will asked.

"Ya, got ya," Jack replied and started to cough again.

The Omega Variant

The Barrio, New York

"Yo, Sammy, what ya got?" Jimmy asked.

"I got rock and tina. The tina is good shit. The Chinese be getting it in here now. They got some way of getting it through the barricades," Sammy replied.

"Okay, give me an 80 of Tina. I got a hookup tonight."

"Good on ya, brother," Sammy replied and coughed a little.

Jimmy took his 80 bag and tucked it away in his special pocket. He hugged it out with Sammy and headed out of the dark, run-down apartment.

As he headed back to his place, he thought about his little world. The Barrio was a red zone. It was because it was poor, Jimmy figured. He had a couple of the vaccine shots so while he didn't have his immunity passport, he felt relatively safe from the virus, even that new Omega variant.

There were benefits of being in a red zone for guys like Jimmy. There were a whole lot fewer cops around. His protection business was growing.

Urban red zones were becoming no-go areas for many people, including the police. Many of the areas, like Jimmy's region, were becoming more gang-managed than government-managed. That didn't bother Jimmy—he was a gang member and made enough money being muscle to live a reasonable life.

As he turned down his street, he could see another burned-out cop car down at the end of it. He smiled. "Fuck the police," he sang to himself as he made his way happily home.

The Omega Variant

The White House, Washington

"So, what are you saying? This one is different?" President Mike Collins asked.

He sat at his desk on the Oval Office with his top aides.

"It does seem to be, Sir. Historically, the mortality has been relatively low with Covid. Initially, it was around 2% but with therapeutics and better medical practices, it reduced to closer to 1%. Additionally, the deaths were disproportionate to the older generation," the chief medical officer, Tom Nelson replied.

"And this new variant, I'm guessing it's different or you wouldn't be here," the president said.

"Yes, it is, sir. This variant, the B.2.7 or the Omega variant, is very different. The mortality rate is closer to 17% and it seems that the rate is consistent across all age bands."

"What about the contagion rate?"

"Similar to the Omicron variant."

"So, this is a real killer."

"Yes sir, it is."

"And the vaccine? How effective is it against this variant?"

"It's early still but the initial research suggests that the mRNA vaccines are still highly effective against this variant assuming you have had all four shots. One more booster vaccine will likely be needed to improve efficacy."

"One more booster. The anti-vax crowd is going to love that."

The president looked over at his vice president. "Jim, we've got a real damn problem here," he said.

"We do, sir," Jim replied.

The president was alluding to the growing resistance to vaccinations across the country. Under the Biden administration, by late 2022, they had effectively beaten Covid, or at least put it at bay. The majority of the country, desperate to regain normality, had elected to do the right thing and get vaccinated.

The issue now was, in addition to Covid fatigue, people felt as if they were protected. Vaccines were old news and the destruction of the truth left behind by the Trump administration and his runs in 2020 and 2024 made it next to impossible to reach a sub-section of America, the one that was most at risk from the new variant.

"Mr. President, the news is covering the new variant already," Jim said.

"I've seen the reports. They don't seem to be onto the mortality rate yet at least," the president replied.

"That will change with the CDC's next update," Jim said.

"We need to be prepared. We need a plan to address this, Jim."

"Mandatory vaccines would be the right thing," Tom said.

"I'm sure they are. The problem here, Tom, is you're talking logic. That's not what the social media chatter is talking about. The folks that need to take this seriously are already calling it fake news. Goddam Trump, he's got these people so brainwashed that they can't even understand the risk that is right in front of them. We'll need to get a team together. Jim, we have to get a handle on this. How many people do we have in those red and yellow zones?"

"Approximately 85 million," he replied.

"And, what was that mortality rate again, Tom?"

"Approximately 17%, sir."

"Jim, do some quick math for me, will you? 17% of 85 million?"

"About 14 million."

The president got up and walked over to the window and looked out.

"Jesus, Jim. We have to find a way to stop this," he said.

The WHO

There was a growing degree of panic at the WHO when the impact of the Omega variant was finally understood.

"Are you saying that the mortality rate is between 16% and 17%?" Director Gonzales asked.

"Yes, in industrial countries. In third-world countries, the rate is over 20%," Hanz Muller, head of research replied.

"Jesus. What about contagion?"

"Similar to Omicron."

"Who else knows about this?" the director asked.

"Well, the core team here, the CDC, the Russians, the Chinese, the EU, England, Canada, Australia, and New Zealand."

Director Gonzales sat quickly for a moment.

"And vaccine protection?" he asked.

"Those fully immunized, by that I mean the four shots, have some protection. With the latest booster, we believe the protection could be as high as 90%. We don't have a lot of data yet."

"We have a lot of people in this world who don't have half that coverage. We need to talk to all the countries. We're going to need to quarantine again. We will need another lockdown," the director replied.

The team in the room all looked down at the floor. They all knew what that meant. Another lockdown was the last thing the world was going to accept, despite how critical this one might just be.

Last Call

Will stood in front of the locked door at Jack's Bar and Grill.

"What the hell man?" Will yelled out as he tugged on the door.

"It's closed," a man sitting on a dusty, run-down old bench said.

"I can see that. Jack's is never closed. Least not in the afternoon," Will replied.

"Well, it's closed today on account of Jack being dead."

Will stopped pulling on the door handle and turned to look at the man.

"What you mean, dead?"

"Dead, you know, gone. He died last night at the hospital. They tell me it was Covid, that new variant, that Omega one."

Will made his way over to the bench and sat down.

"Heck, man. Covid is bullshit. Who are you?"

"I'm his brother Dave. You can think whatever you want about this whole virus thing but I'll tell ya, it killed Jack."

Will looked down and dug in the sand a little with his feet.

"I dunno. We keep hearing different things about it, you know. Why are you here anyway?"

"Waiting for the lawyer to come so we can take stock."

Will looked momentarily at Dave and then down at the dusty dirt again.

"Shit, I'm sorry, man. I just saw him two days ago. He had a little cough, is all. He was a good guy."

"Ya, he was."

Will turned and looked up at the sign on the front of the bar.

"This was home for me. I don't know what I'm going to do now," he said.

Dave turned, looked at him, but said nothing.

Will got up and slowly walked back to his pickup.

A New Old Policy

The American administration, working with the CDC and the WHO, did develop a policy to deal with the Omega variant. It wasn't rocket science; it was based on the tried-and-true policies that had been effective in battling Covid since 2020.

It was simple, at least on the surface. An awareness campaign, updated to reflect the high mortality rate, mobile vaccine campaign, testing, tracking, masks, and some level of a shutdown. It had all been done before, successfully.

The challenge this time was that the policy was primarily targeted at that sticky 30%, the group that had steadfastly stuck to the belief that Covid wasn't real and the vaccine was a government program to control them. It was no surprise since the Trump 2024 campaign had reaffirmed that belief.

The initial news on the mortality rate of the variant was met with skepticism in many places and downright disbelief in the areas that would likely be most affected.

Vaccine rates did not move much until the dead bodies began to pile up. As was the case through previous waves, deaths trailed cases by about three weeks. A few weeks after cases shot up, the deaths followed and the reality of the variant began to set in. For the first time since the Civil War, there were bodies in the streets.

The administration's response was to push their mobile units into the red zones and set up large-scale vaccinations.

They initially found hesitation, then resistance. Ultimately, despite the growing death toll, the resistance mounted to the point where vaccination sites and mobile units came under fire, literally.

The authorities in those areas did their best to contain the growing violence but the efforts were ineffective. Part of the problem was that the local authorities often shared the general mindset of the counties. Why wouldn't they? They were family, friends, and neighbors after all.

The administration tried to provide protective services but it found itself hamstrung, not unlike January 6th, 2021. America had spent years preparing for foreign combatants while consistently underestimating the real risk at home. Local militia in red zones slowly began to take over. From there it wasn't a long slide to civil war.

A Proper Funeral

Bobby was starting to realize just how lucky he was. Luck, however, might not have been the best choice of words given that he had just lost his wife.

He had been able to arrange a full funeral for his wife, Lilly. In the three days since her death, the number of deaths had gone through the roof.

The local news had announced earlier in the day that all deaths going forward would have to forego funerals. There simply wasn't enough capacity to handle it. Bodies were to be burned.

Lafayette wasn't a big city. The city proper had about 125,000 folks, while the metropolitan area was closer to half a million. It was a small- to mid-size city with an infrastructure appropriate for that.

The hospitals had become overrun the day after Lilly's death. For those who became sick from that day on, there was nowhere to go. Most of Louisiana was a red zone. It didn't matter where you were, you got sick, you were screwed. So when Bobby walked into his church, he was grateful.

"Father, I do appreciate you taking the time today for the funeral. I know it's a difficult time," Bobby said as he shook Father Matthews' hand.

"Son, it is in difficult times like this that we all need to turn to the Lord. It is his light that will guide us through this challenge," Father Matthews replied.

"Yes, you are right. So, we will see you this afternoon at 2 pm then," Bobby said.

"Yes, son. All is arranged."

"Oh, Father, one last question. Are masks required today?"

"Of course not, son. We are all bathed in Jesus' blood here."

"Good. That is what I expected. Just some folks were asking, you know."

"Of course. See you at 2," Father Matthews said and went back inside the church.

As he drove home, Bobby thought about what the father had said. *Bathed in Jesus' blood.* For some reason, it didn't seem to apply to Lilly, despite her faith in God. He shook the thought off. He was grieving and carrying some guilt, he knew that. Lilly had suggested getting the vaccine a couple of times over the last few years. It was he and his father who were adamant that no one in the family was going to get any vaccines.

Sadly, his father was now sick too, very sick.

He arrived back at his house he found family and many loved ones. They had come to support the family, as people do in times of need. He made his way through the partially crowded house. He noticed that there were many missing friends and family.

"Bobby, how are you holding up?" his uncle, George, asked.

"I'm doing alright, I guess. Worried about Pop. He's sick now too."

"Ya, I was just in to see him at his place earlier. He don't look too good. I guess there's no way of getting him into a hospital."

"No. Everything is shut down. Can't even get someone to come by."

"We got too many people sick, Bobby. That's the problem."

Bobby looked around the living room. He was curious to see who was watching him. It seemed that everyone was engrossed in their own discussions. He looked back at Uncle George.

"You believe this whole Covid thing?" Bobby asked.

"I dunno. When it first started, I was with everyone else around here. Seemed that it was a big plan to get rid of Trump. I gotta say, with everything going on now, I don't know anymore."

The thought George just echoed was exactly where Bobby's thinking had gotten to. He wasn't sure what he believed anymore. He had just watched his wife die and of something the doctor was convinced was avoidable. He could still hear the doctor's words after she died. *Bobby, this didn't have to happen. Do the right thing for you and your children.*

"I always thought Trump knew things that the government didn't want people to know. He seemed to want to fix things, you know, for folks like us."

"Ya, he did but with all the stuff going down now, I kinda think he was full of shit," Uncle George said.

Ya me too, Bobby thought. He wasn't, however, quite ready to say it out loud.

"Hey, Uncle George, I'll catch up with you in a bit," Bobby said and patted George on the back.

He knew his mother would still be at her house, watching over his father. He would go and gather her in time for the funeral but he did need to speak with the people who had come to pay their respects. It was better that she wasn't there. He did not want to put the burden of a gathering on her at this point.

He knew a few of the conversations were going to be difficult. Some of Lilly's friends had already been vocal about their feelings that she didn't have to die. They were advocates for vaccinations and were adamant that had Lilly had them, she'd still be alive.

Bobby never believed that. For him, the vaccination had been all about government tracking and control. In his opinion, the vaccine would have made no difference at all.

The Omega Variant

He managed to avoid the group before making his exit. He drove over to his parent's place to get his mother and daughters.

He pulled onto the driveway to see his daughters sitting out on the porch.

"Daddy!" the younger daughter, Sasha, yelled as Bobby got out of the car.

Sasha, followed by her older sister, Sarah, came running down to meet him.

"Girls, what's going on? Why are you outside?" Bobby asked.

"Daddy, Grandpa is really sick. He won't stop coughing and is making strange sounds with his breaths," Sasha said.

"Is he going to die?" Sarah asked.

"Hell no. You know Grandpa, nothing can kill him," Bobby said as he picked Sasha up.

"Good, I love Grandpa," Sarah replied.

"Come on, let's go get Grandma."

They made their way into the house and Bobby plunked the two girls down on the couch.

"I'll go get Grandma. You guys wait here," he said.

He headed to the bedroom where he found his mother sitting on a chair by the bed where his father lay sleeping.

"How is he, Mom?" Bobby asked.

"He's not good, Bobby. I'm really worried about him. He's gotten a lot worse since yesterday. He keeps saying it's not Covid but I don't know. He's never been this sick, Bobby," she said.

Bobby went over to the bed and looked at his dad. It was true he didn't look good. In fact, he looked terrible. He looked just as Lilly did before they finally took her to the hospital.

"I'm sure he'll be fine. You know how Dad is."

"I wish we could take him to the hospital."

"It didn't do any good for Lilly."

"Maybe. We used to go to the hospital for these things and now it's all messed up. I don't care about what is right or wrong or left or right. I know you all watch Fox and they have been telling people not to worry, but I do. I just want things the way they were again. It seems to me that the world ain't working right anymore," she replied emotionally.

Bobby decided that it wasn't the time to argue about such things.

"Mom, we have to go. Dad will be okay while we're gone, he's sleeping," he said.

She bent over, kissed her husband's head, and replied, "Yes, I know."

Bobby pulled the blanket up onto his father and bid him goodbye for the time being.

They all headed out to the car and made their way to the church.

When they arrived at the church, they found several protesters outside. It seemed that those who were not able to arrange for funerals were not pleased with the situation. They were, however, respectful of those who were remembering a family member that day.

Bobby and his family entered the church and found his brother, Billy, waiting inside.

"Bobby, good that you are here. Father Matthews is ready to start. He says he has a very busy day with funerals today," Billy said.

"Thanks, Billy. I appreciate you being here. I stopped by to see Dad on the way," Bobby replied as they entered the church.

"How is he?"

"Not good."

"Jesus, I hope we're not back here again."

"Me either. I have to find the priest. I'll catch up with you later."

Bobby left his brother and found Father Matthews. They agreed to get the precession started.

From there, Bobby found his daughters, his brother, and his mother and joined them. He looked around the pews. It seemed to him that there was only about half the number of people he was expecting.

"Where is everybody?" Bobby whispered to his brother.

"I heard that many are sick or scared to get sick," Billy whispered back.

Despite the smaller than expected gathering, the funeral was wonderfully done and touching. In the end, the crowd gathered together and followed the priest and the casket out to the adjacent cemetery.

The shining sun belied the horror that was taking place under it. Bobby had never seen so many fresh graves. The cemetery seemed to have maxed out its availability. The dead with so many stories to tell.

At the gravesite, Father Matthews walked through the classic words once the casket found the bottom of the grave.

As Bobby and his daughters tossed earth down, someone was overheard yelling, "Shame, shame on you. She didn't have to die."

Bobby looked up to see Ally pointing at him. She was quickly hushed and led away by others who were there. It was, however, too late as both his daughters picked up on what was said.

"Daddy, what did she mean Mommy didn't have to die?" Sarah asked.

"It's nothing, Sarah. She is just very upset about Mommy. Can you two stay with grandma while I say goodbye to people?" Bobby asked.

Both girls smiled and said, "Yes."

Bobby made his way around the gathering and thanked everyone. Fortunately, Lilly's three friends, including Ally, had left.

He thanked Father Matthews, gathered his two daughters, his mother, and headed to the car.

The drive back to his mother's house was not unexpectedly quiet. Seeing body backs in front of houses had that effect. When they arrived, Bobby had the two girls wait in the car while he walked his mother in.

"Bobby, please come with me to check on your father before you go," his mother asked.

"Of course, Mom."

They headed down the hall to the master bedroom. When they entered the room, Bobby immediately sensed something was wrong. There was an air of death.

"Mom, let me check on Dad, okay," he said.

He went to the side of the bed and bent down to his father. There was no breathing. He put his fingers to his father's neck and found no pulse.

He pulled the blanket up over his father's face, turned to his mother, and said, "I'm sorry, he's gone."

Battle Lines

Come late fall 2025, the Omega variant was in full rage around the world. The public had become aware of the mortality rate and while some called it fake news, it was hard to dispute with facts when bodies were piling up.

In the dead zones, as the red zones became known, bodies literally began to pile up. It was inevitable. In some red zone counties, the unvaccinated or under-vaccinated were as high as 50%. They were the same segment of the population that staunchly believed that their rights superseded any responsibility and the prevailing conspiracy of the day.

The combination was deadly. Some counties had infection rates hit 40% or more. Ultimately, it became hard to even measure as many of the testing sites were forced to close down due to the violence and a lack of tests. The Republican Congress had targeted slowing down testing early in 2025 and had canceled many of the government contracts.

Hospitals in those zones became overrun, and quickly. In some places, the medical staff had had enough. Many of them had lived through 2020, 2021, and 2022 and just couldn't do it anymore.

Eventually, citizens were forced to band together in the hardest-hit areas to manage the dead. Initially, it was done in a sympathetic manner where priests and other clergies would preside over rushed funeral services. When the daily dead outnumbered the funeral capacity, chaos set in.

In scenes reminiscent of the black plague, trucks were mobilized to collect the dead and bring them to mass grave sites where the bodies were burned on a nightly basis.

Families initially protested but the new local authorities took control. The new authorities in many cases in the south were a mix of Proud Boys, Oath Keepers, the Three Percenters, and other militia groups. In some places they had the support of the police, in others, they simply outnumbered them.

The borders between red and green counties, originally managed by American reserves, were quickly augmented on both sides by local militias. Those on the green side were keeping people out. On the red side, they were keeping people in and the government out.

With the availability of military-grade weapons to the American public, a deep divide in philosophy, and the terror of daily mass deaths, it wasn't long before a battle was brewing.

A Barrio in Flames

Jimmy figured he had waited long enough. He knew it was Sammy's corner, it had been for years and, given it was Friday night, there was no reason for Sammy not to be there, so he walked over to the dark man who was there.

"Yo, where's Sammy?" Jimmy asked the man.

"He ain't here no more," the man replied.

"I see that. Why the fuck ain't he here?" Jimmy said annoyed.

"He ain't here on account of him being dead."

The answer caught Jimmy a little off guard. It probably should not have. There was certainly a lot of death around but somehow Jimmy always figured the guys like him and Sammy, guys who lived on the fringes of society, were somehow excluded from the problems of the regular world. How could a little virus kill them off?

"Shit, man, I didn't know."

"Don't worry about it. Just happened yesterday. It's my corner now. You can call me Eddy. What do you need?"

"Gram of tina."

"That's $100 brother."

"You're shitting me. Last week I could get two grams for $80."

"Ya, well, that was last week. We got supply problems now with everything being locked down tight. Take it or leave it. One way or another, I'll sell it to someone tonight."

Jimmy rummaged through his pocket. He had exactly $112. Money had gotten tight; everything had gotten tight since the increased lockdown. The pandemic, which had been a boom to business initially, was now becoming a bust.

"Fuck yeah, I'll take it," he handed over the $100 and pocketed the tina.

He headed back to his place. As he walked, he could see flames across the horizon and could smell the smoke in the air. Smoke from fires and the burning of bodies.

"Shit, I gotta get out of here," he mumbled as he walked.

Mounting Concern

As Jim listened to the daily update from his team, he shuddered. Things were, unfortunately, playing out exactly as their latest modeling had predicted and it was a dire prediction.

"How the hell is this thing so deadly? How many variants have we had in the last four years? The one consistency was the mortality rate. It's never been above 2%. 17% is way out of scope. It's almost as if this is a completely different virus," Jim grumbled.

"Sir, if I may, while this variant uses the same, known methodology to attach to cells within the respiratory system, there are some major differences in the way this variant replicates once attached inside the body. Its growth cycle is essentially on steroids," the Chief Medical Office replied.

"How is that possible? How could a virus naturally mutate so significantly?"

"It generally doesn't. Not this fast at least. A mutation such as this would normally take many years to develop to this stage."

"So, what's happening here?"

"I can't say with certainty but we seem to be facing a one-of-a-kind variant. It appears to have learned from its predecessors. This learning or evolving is not uncommon but the efficiency of Covid and this variant, in particular, is unheard of."

Jim looked around the table. The team was the best of the best from medical, to legal, to military, and logistics. He was looking to see if what the Chief Medical Officer had said shocked others aside from himself. The looks on the face confirmed it.

"So, we're dealing with an intelligent virus. I need you guys to figure out how the hell how to get ahead of the thing," Jim said and then got up and left the room.

Fake News

With Jack's Bar and Grill shutdown, Will needed a new hangout. His days were free since he had been on disability for the last three years. Add to that a little bit of money he inherited when his father died, and he had kissed his working days behind some time ago.

He knew a few other spots not too far from his place so he hopped in his pickup and headed out.

He drove along a favorite local road. He had the radio on, country and western, he was tired of talk radio. He remembered a good old bar and grill somewhere along the route.

After about ten minutes in the pickup, he spotted it. Bill's Bar and Grill. Not much of a name but, given the pickups parked outside, it looked like a good enough place to him.

He parked and headed into the bar. It was around 2 pm and a good dozen or so folks were sitting in the run-down, smokey place.

Will made his way up to the bar and grabbed a stool.

"What can I get ya?" the bartender said.

"Bud Light."

"I got ya," the bartender replied and reached into the fridge.

The bartender slid him a lukewarm bottle of beer.

He looked around the bar. It wasn't much different than Jack's place was—just a different set of regulars, he figured.

He pulled out his pack of smokes and put one in his mouth.

"Hey, mind if I grab one too, buddy?" a man two seats down asked.

Will looked over at him. He was a big man, a little Hispanic in him it seemed, mid-thirties, and a bit rough around the edges.

"Yeah, no worries," he replied.

"You new here?"

"Yup. Used to hang over at Jack's bar."

"So why you come here?"

"Jack died. Place is closed down now."

"Shit, man, a lot of people been dying lately. I'm Carlos. I'm a trucker but I ain't got no work now cause they closed off travel cross counties if you ain't vaccinated."

"It's them fucking Greens. They are doing this to try and control us," an older man at the end of the bar shouted out.

"Damn right about that," Will replied.

"I dunno, Earl. A lot of people are indeed dying. Maybe there's some truth in this Omega thing. I ain't never seen so many people sick and the hospital by my place can't take any more sick folk," the bartender said.

"Come on Pete, it's all fake news. You heard Tucker; he says they're writing everything down as Covid as they did in 2020. He also says that the vaccine might be what's killing some folks," Earl replied.

"No one really knows what in that thing. No way I'm ever taking one of them needles," Carlos said.

"I guess you're okay with dying," a woman in the corner said.

The bar got quiet. Everyone turned to see a well-dressed middle-aged woman sitting at a table with a well-dressed middle-aged man.

"Why do you think you can say that in here?" Carlos said aggressively.

"I think I'm qualified to speak here. I used to be an immunology researcher for the government until they shut the facility down here."

"What the fuck is immunologic?" Earl asked.

"It's the study of viruses and diseases," she casually replied.

"So, you telling us the Covid is real. That ain't what other people is saying," Carlos said.

She laughed and took a sip of her drink.

"I'm guessing Tim and I are the only ones who are immune here. I'm not going to argue with you guys. The rate things are going, we'll be the only ones from this bar left alive in afew weeks."

Carlos stood up abruptly and started to approach the woman's table. "Maybe you won't survive neither," he said.

"Now, Carlos, settle down or I'm gonna have to toss you out again," the bartender said.

Carlos stood for a moment staring at the woman and Tim and then sat back down.

She smiled and said, "Don't worry, big guy, we're on our way out anyway. We just stopped for a quick drink on the road. We're leaving this county because we can."

The two of them got up, paid their bill, and walked out. As she walked out, she looked back and said, "Good luck. It's not too late to get vaccinated. It might just save your life."

"Fuck you, Greenies!" Will shouted.

Carlos stood up again and patted Will on the back. "Good to have ya here, Will," he said.

Will smiled and ordered another Bud Light. Just like that, he had found himself a new home, just like the old one.

Burying Dad

Bobby took the girls and his mother back to his home and called his uncle to come over to watch the kids. He needed to head back to his mother's house to sort out his father's death.

Along the way back, he reflected on how the world around him was changing so rapidly. They had survived six waves of Covid without any real issues. Sure, he and Lilly had gotten sick with the Delta variant back in 2021 but it wasn't much more than a really bad cold.

This one, somehow, seemed different. He drove along the old familiar route but this time, it felt different. The scent in the air was a mix of the dead rotting in homes where no one had found them and the nightly body burn.

Shit, what the hell had happened? Covid, if it was real, was supposed to pass. Hell, even the Spanish flu passed but this damn thing just would not go away. What Bobby didn't realize was the virus hung around because of people like him. He and the other unvaccinated had provided the perfect ongoing breeding ground for variants and nature was perfecting it.

As he drove, he called his brother and asked him to come to meet him at the house.

Bobby arrived a few minutes later and went in. The odor of death was growing. He went to his parent's room and sat down in the chair in the corner.

He looked around the room. It was the house he, they, had grown up in. The one house his parents had shared for their married entire life. Now it was a morgue.

As he sat, he was flooded with memories, ones from the early years in particular. He remembered rising with the sun where he and his brother would crash his parent's bed. He remembered how the light would cut in through the old drapes that hung by the window and they would lie in its warmth and talk.

His father was his hero, his teacher, his mentor. Now he lay dead upon the same bed. He worried that, just maybe, his father had misguided him in the end.

He heard the door open and a moment later his brother Billy walked in.

"Damn. Is that Dad?" he asked.

"Yeah."

"You sure he's dead?"

"Oh yeah."

Billy got up and went to look at his father. He pulled the sheet back and gasped.

"Yup, he's real dead," he said.

Bobby stood up and looked. His father was well into rigor mortis. The man he knew was gone.

"Shit, Bobby, what the hell we gonna do about this?" Billy asked.

"I dunno."

"Well, we know Dad didn't wanna be burned."

Bobby thought about that comment for a moment. A piece of him was angry. Angry at his dad, angry at the world, angry at God. He had just buried his wife and now he had to worry about what his dead father wanted or didn't want.

"You know we can't get a funeral. All that shit is closed down. What else are we gonna do?" Bobby replied.

Billy looked around the room. "Maybe we could just bury him in the woods."

"Yeah, maybe," Bobby said undecidedly.

"What's the matter with you? Pop is dead and you just sitting there," Billy asked.

"I just buried my wife and people are saying she didn't have to die. Maybe she didn't. Maybe Pop was wrong about all this shit."

"Bobby, you don't really believe that, do you?"

"I don't know what to believe no more. People are dying all over, just like the government said."

Bobby rocked back in the chair for moment.

"Fine, let's wrap Pop up real good with blankets and we'll bury him in that field down by the old river. We'll just bring Mom, the kids, and a few cousins," Bobby replied.

"I guess that works. I'll go get some blankets," Billy said.

Bobby got up and joined him.

They returned and carefully wrapped their father. He was light, much lighter than in his heyday when he was a big man. His frame had been hollowed by Covid over the last few weeks. It was not the way Bobby wanted to remember him.

Once they were done, they brought him to the basement as it was the coolest place in the house.

They then headed to the garage and grabbed a couple of shovels.

Billy led the way to the riverside and together they picked out a spot. It was in a place where they had all spent time together in their lives. After some forty minutes or so of digging under a warm November sun, they had a reasonable grave prepared.

"Alright, let's go get the family," Bobby said, and the two of them hiked their way back to the house.

Getting Out of Town

Jimmy sat drinking a beer at one of the only drinking holes still open in the Barrio, a dive called Hernando's Hideaway.

"Yo, Jimmy, what you doing here at this hour of the day?" a voice from behind him asked.

He turned to see an old friend, Big Al.

"Shit Big Al, where else I'm gonna be doing? There ain't no work right now. Everything is shutting down."

"Yeah, I know. I got tossed last week too. Nobody needs a bouncer when your bar is closed."

"Yup, that's pretty much it."

Big Al sat down and ordered a beer.

"Hey, do you got the vaccines?" Big Al asked.

Jimmy turned to look at him, somewhat surprised by the question.

"I had the two shots back in '21 but never did the follow-up boosters."

"Yeah, same with me. I kinda think maybe we should have gotten them."

Jimmy took a sip from his beer. "Yeah, kinda thinking the same thing."

Big Al took a swig from his beer and looked around the room.

"You know there are still a lot of folks who think this Omega virus thing is fake and that the government is using it to get people to take the vaccine. They say the vaccine will control you," Big Al said.

Jimmy laughed.

"Ya, I hear that too. I kinda think that ain't true."

"Me either. People are dying all over. You know my cousin, Maurice, he died yesterday. No funeral, nothing. The government just came and took his body away."

"That's fucked up."

"No kidding. He couldn't even get into the hospital. They got no more room. They told me they burned his body."

"I hear that too."

Big Al slid his chair closer to Jimmy.

"You know I'm thinking about getting that new booster but there are only a few spots that got it and it's hard to get in."

Jimmy already knew that. He had looked as well over the last few days. It seemed that a lot of people were thinking the same thing. The real problem was availability. The government had ramped down the vaccine clinics the year before, citing low demand. Now with the travel restrictions, given that they were in a red zone, it was hard for the government to bring supplies into the area, not to mention demand globally had skyrocketed.

"Yeah, I tried a couple of places the other day. Huge lineups or no supply," Jimmy replied.

"I hear you. Hey, I got a friend who says he can get me the super booster, black market. 500 bucks he says."

"Shit, that's steep."

"Damn right and, given I ain't got no work, it doesn't matter, I can't afford."

500 dollars, Jimmy thought. In good times he could pull that off but these weren't good times. He felt frustrated that he should have to pay for something that should be free but he knew somehow things got messed up along the way. America was messed up. He was a simple man but he was starting to see the danger in all the bullshit news that had been thrust upon them over the last few years. He was pretty sure every politician and media person from CNN to Fox was fully vaccinated. Talk on the media channels was just that, talk. It was all done for their audience.

"Shit, I ain't got 500 bucks either," Jimmy replied.

Big Al shifted in his chair. Jimmy could hear the chair creak under his weight. He looked around this time as if looking to see if anyone was listening.

"Jimmy, I got another way. Me and some guys are thinking about getting out of here. Not just the Barrio but out of the whole place, out of America, you know. We thinking of going up to Canada. They got things right there. Everybody's immune and they even got free medical stuff. We're working on a plan."

Shit, Canada. Jimmy had always liked Canada. He had visited his cousin years ago with his family up in Toronto. It was so clean, so safe, that he found it fascinating.

"That sounds good. Can I get in with you guys?" Jimmy asked.

"Yeah, I think that would be cool. We could use a guy like you. I'll check with the guys and let you know."

"Thanks, bro. Hey, I got to get going. Let me know what's up with this," Jimmy said and finished off his beer.

The two of them got up and hugged.

As Jimmy walked out of the bar, he took his phone out and saw that he had a message. It was from his sister. It simply read: Call me, Mom just died.

The New Militia

It was a warm, dry early November Texas afternoon and Will was happily sitting in his new air-conditioned hangout, with his new friends when a couple of guys armed with AR-15s and dressed in fatigues walked in.

"How y'all doing? I'm Rick and we are with the new local militia. Me and Tim here are Proud Boys and we are part of the new Texas militia. We are recruiting folks to help us man the county border," Rick said.

Will looked over at Carlos and smiled.

"Shit, man where do I sign up?" Carlos said and stood up.

Will stood up behind him as did several other men.

"I knew we came into the right bar. Come over the corner here and Tim and I will walk you through what's going on," Rick said.

Will, Carlos, and three others happily made their way to the corner.

"So what we got going on is that the government wants to control us," Rick started.

"You got that right," Will said.

"Anyways, word is that the government is gonna try and come in with that vaccine and force us to take it," Rick said.

"Well fuck that, we ain't taking it," Carlos replied

"No, we ain't. By the way, any of you got the vaccine? It's a showstopper for us."

All five men vigorously confirmed they hadn't.

"Alright, that's good. As you'll know, the main routes in and out of our county are already controlled from the outside. What we are doing is setting control points on our side of the border. We don't want them fuckers coming in here," Rick said.

"What about the police? Shouldn't they be doing that?" one of the other men asked.

"A lot of them are with us already. They told us they won't interfere with us. Now, you all got a gun?" Rick asked.

Four of the five of them confirmed they did.

"I gotta admit that I don't cause of my criminal record," one of the men said.

"Brother, if you join the new militia, we'll take care of you," Tim replied.

The man smiled. Will and Carlos patted him on the back. They were all family now.

"Now we gotta get you signed up if you are ready for it," Rick said.

"Yeah, give me that damn pen," Carlos said.

Just like that, a bunch of drunks was about to become part of the new militia.

A Sad Goodbye

Bobby and his family pulled up to the house. Some of the cousins were already there waiting. Bobby got out of the car and greeted them while Billy got their mother out of the car.

"Geez, Bobby, I'm so sorry this happened and on the day of Lilly's funeral. We got too much bad in the world right now," his Uncle George said.

"It's been a tough day all around," Bobby replied.

"It has, son. Come, let's get this ceremony underway, or else we're gonna run out of daylight."

Bobby, Billy, and the family made their way into the house and to the living room.

"I know it has been a hard day for everyone. When God calls us, it's our time. Sadly, God has called two of our families in short order. We don't have the luxury of a proper funeral today so we are going to bury Dad in a spot Billy and I picked out by the river that Dad loved. So people, family, let's get going. I'd like to ask a couple of cousins to join Billy and me in carrying Dad down to the river," Bobby said.

Uncle George and his son Melvin quickly stepped up and offered to help.

Just as the group was about to set out, Sarah asked, quite loudly, "Daddy, why didn't we just get vaccinated?"

With all eyes on him, Bobby quietly replied, "We can talk about that later."

Bobby, Billy, Uncle George, and cousin Melvin headed down to the basement to retrieve their father.

"Wow, he's pretty light," Melvin said.

Uncle George glared at him.

"Shit, I'm sorry," Melvin said.

"That's okay, Melvin. He is light now. His time has passed. Remember him as he was," Bobby said and smiled at him.

"I will, Bobby."

The four men carefully carried Bobby's father up the stairs, through the house, and out the back door.

They all walked somberly against the late day sun down to the spot that Bobby and Merv had selected earlier in the day.

When they arrived, the four men carefully lowered Bobby's father into the grave that they had dug earlier.

When they were done, Uncle George stood at top of the grave and said a few words. He finished with the traditional dust to dust and tossed some earth down into the grave.

Once he was done, the rest of them all joined in and filled the grave handful by handful.

As they were walking back, Sarah grabbed her father's hand and they walked quietly together. As they approached the house, she began to cough violently.

A Difficult Update

"Jim, what do you have for us?" the president asked.

"Frankly, not good news, sir. The latest data confirms this thing is a real killer. If we are to get through this thing, we need to roll out a massive rapid vaccination program. We need to bring the unvaccinated up-to-date and get the super booster to those who had the original two shots. We have prepared a strategic plan with FEMA and the Pentagon," Jim replied.

The president looked closely at Jim. "Jim, I've known you for years. I know that tone. I appreciate the plan but I sense something else in your message," he said.

Jim picked up his papers and looked from one end of the table to the other. It was the who's who of American politics and military.

"We have a significant challenge with local resistance. More than that, the armed local militia have been taking up control points in red counties across the country. It's more acute in the southern regions. You know the players, Proud Boys, Oath Keepers, and others. They have gained some pretty strategic ground over the last few months."

"Are you telling me that we can't get vaccines into these areas?"

"For some of the regions, it seems so, sir."

"Damn it. Do these people realize they are gonna die? I know we've had issues in the past but I would think with the severity of Omega people would welcome the vaccine. General Anderson, what options do we have to push into these areas?"

"It's complicated. First, we have the constitutional limitation where we can't deploy the U.S. military on American soil so any action would have to be led by the National Guard. The problem we have with that is that a portion of the National Guard has defected, or is sick in the regions where we need them," General Anderson replied.

"Jim, let me guess. If I were to ask Congress to allow an exemption to the military order, it would get shot down," the president asked.

"Given the Republican majority, most certainly."

"What about an executive order?"

"It would be outside the scope of executive orders, given the fact that it would contravene the constitution."

"Here we are, trying to help people and we can't. What has this country become? Frankly, I don't know if I recognize it anymore."

"I don't disagree with you, sir," Jim said.

The president looked around the table and then down for a moment.

"Jim, let's get the GOP in here and see if we can't figure out a bipartisan solution," he said.

"Yes, sir. I had anticipated that and am already reaching out."

"Thank you, Jim. Thank all of you. May God bless us," the president said.

The president collected his papers and left the room. As he did, he briefly looked up and wondered if God gave a shit at that point.

An Escape Plan

When Jimmy got to his place he called his sister.

"Kim, I just got your message. Mom's dead? What happened?" he asked.

"Yes, she is. It's really sad. She got sick a few days ago. She got really sick, fast, and then when I checked on her this afternoon, she was dead."

"Shit, so fast. She had the two shots that we had back in '21. I thought that gave some protection."

"Well, it seems that it doesn't. Mom wasn't healthy so that didn't help either."

"Is there going to be a funeral?"

"Yes, I'm working on the details."

Jimmy thought about his sister. They were not particularly close but he liked and respected her. She was alone with their Mother. Their father had passed and she was divorced. He wanted to help her; the problem was he was in a red zone and she was in a green zone.

"Sis, you know I want to help but it's hard as hell to get out of this zone," he said.

She started to cry. "I know. That's why I told you last year after they set that whole zone thing up that you need to start the process to get out. You always do the easy thing, the lazy thing, and there you are now," she said.

He didn't answer. He knew she was right. He had made it to Dad's funeral but that was before, before the borders were set up.

"I'm sorry, Jimmy. I'm just upset. There is a government process that should make it easier for you to come here. I looked into it—it's for bereavement. You need to apply online. I could use your help."

He knew that. He could hear it in her voice. "Okay, send me the link and I'll apply for it," he said.

"Alright, I'll send it over to you a little later. I have to get over to one of the funeral homes and make some arrangements."

"Okay, we'll talk later."

He hung up and grabbed a beer out of the fridge. He went and crashed on the couch. He turned the TV on and sat back.

It was Thursday night. Normally it would be a big night out for him but he was broke. So there he was, sitting on the couch with a Bud Light.

A little later, he grabbed his old laptop and checked his email. There was one from his sister with the link she had mentioned.

He put his beer down and followed the link. He filled in the information and clicked 'Apply'. A few seconds later, 'Declined' popped up on the screen. He clicked on the link that gave the explanation. He was rejected based on his past criminal record.

He slammed the top shut and went and grabbed another beer.

As he sat back on the couch, his phone rang.

"Yo, It's Big Al. I talked to the boys. You're in if you want." Big Al said.

Jimmy looked down at the laptop and said, "Damn right I'm in."

Basic Training

Will showed up at the address that he was given by Rick and Tim and found several dozen other men there as well.

Will parked his pickup, got out, and grabbed his AR-15 off the gun rack in the back of the truck.

As he wandered over to where the men were gathering, he noticed how the AR-15 was very much the gun of choice.

When he reached the group, one of the men held his gun over his head and yelled out, "God bless America."

Will and most of the rest of them followed suit and lifted their guns above their heads. As a group, they shouted out, "Amen."

They spent a few minutes getting to know each other when the militia leaders came and joined them.

"Welcome, welcome to making America great," one of them said to a round of yeehaw.

"First things first. We gonna have to have y'all do a little paperwork. So, follow me over to that building over there and you'll be deputized," he said.

They all toed the line and followed the man into what was essentially a barn. Inside, they lined up and, in turn, each signed a series of papers. They were told the documents were to cover roles and responsibilities and had the needed disclaimers in them.

Will, like the rest of them, briefly looked them over before eagerly signing.

Once the paperwork was done, they went on to be deputized. A local sheriff was there and, one by one, he enlisted them. He also made it very clear that they were part of a new volunteer force, meaning they would not be paid or compensated in any way.

With the logistics done, the group was taken to another building. The armory, they were told it was called. When they got inside it was clear why it was named that way.

"Jesus, look at this place," one of the guys said as they all looked around.

The building housed all sorts of weapons from handguns to rifles to some military-grade gear. The recruits were mostly quiet as they all looked around in envy of what was there.

One of the militia leaders stepped forward and, watching the faces of recruits, laughed.

"Gentlemen, you all feel you are in the right place?" he asked.

Among a chorus of cheers, Will yelled out, "Hell yeah."

He then noticed Carlos was there as well and he made his way over to join him.

"This is the real deal, Will," Carlos said as Will approached.

"Damn straight. Glad those guys came into our bar."

"Yeah, me too."

"Alright gentlemen, the fun is over for now. Follow me to the briefing room," the leader said.

Like excited schoolchildren, they all followed in line. They were led into a side room where chairs had been set up and there was a podium in the front.

As they all sat, the man who had led them in took to the podium. "Welcome recruits. Welcome to making our America great," he said to a huge cheer.

"Today we are going to run you all through our mandate and our role in fixing our part of the country. Our government has abandoned us. It is our time to rise!" he shouted, fist in the air.

The twenty-five or so men all stood and cheered.

The leader waved them back down to their seats. He then walked them through the group's history and how they were now a unification of several militias with similar views and were many thousand strong. He explained that they were becoming the new police and military within a group of counties, all sharing the same red designation.

He went on to say they were going to set up control points around the four counties where they would be controlling access in and out. He was asked why they would be controlling people leaving the county. He replied saying they needed to keep a level population to run the economy. People seemed to get that.

He finished by explaining the roles of the recruits. They would undergo a weekend training program and then be assigned to border shifts. The borders were to be expanded from major roads to any roads: side and dirt.

Most of the recruits were to be assigned to these side roads once they were done with the training.

In the end, none of them really cared where they would be assigned. All they cared about was that they were playing a role in making their corner of America better.

Infection

Bobby bid the friends and family who had attended their private little service goodbye and got his kids and his mother into the car. There was no way his mother was going to stay in the old house. Not in the bed his father had just died in.

As they drove back, Sarah continued to cough in the back seat.

"Daddy, I don't feel good," she said.

"Let's get you home and we'll sort you out, sweetie," he replied.

He quietly picked up the pace. He was concerned, very concerned. How could he not be? He had just lost his wife and his father. He was starting to think the whole Covid hoax thing was maybe not quite true. The problem was that the reality came at a tremendous cost.

They arrived home and Bobby helped Sarah into the house. Once inside, he got her some cough syrup and put her to bed.

When he returned to the living room, he found his mother and Sasha staring at him.

"Okay, what is it?" he asked as he sat down.

"Daddy, Mommy got sick and died. Grandpa got sick and died. Now Sarah is sick. I love her, Daddy. I don't want her to die too," Sasha said and started to cry.

His mother comforted her. "For bloody Christ, Bobby. How many of your family do you want to sit back and watch die? Your father would not let me speak my mind but he is dead now. Dead because he was stubborn. Do you really want to lose your daughters too? Haven't you lost enough?" she yelled at him.

He sunk back into his recliner. It was his old comfort zone but it was a long way from comforting at that point.

"What do you want me to do?"

"Be a man, Bobby. Save your daughters before it's too late."

A Bipartisan Challenge

"Mr. President, we have the GOP team waiting outside the Oval Office," Jim said as he poked his head into the room.

The president looked around the room. He had the Democratic brain trust as well as the nation's leaders in health, logistics, and military.

"Let's head over to the briefing room," the president replied.

Jim and the president joined the group outside the Oval Office and led them to the briefing room.

In a scene reminiscent of so many crises before his time, he looked around the briefing room, at the faces of those there. He knew there were crises that somehow, through thick or thin, America had successfully battled through.

This was his moment now. It was his turn in a long cycle of challenges and the truth was he was scared.

"Folks, we all know why we are here. We have a serious crisis on our hands and we need to find a bipartisan solution if this country is going to survive. Now, before you all start talking, I want us all to hear, together, the critical updates. Some of you will likely have heard parts of this based on what committees you are on but I want all of us to be on the same page before the negotiations start," the president said.

Jim stepped out of the room briefly and returned with the medical team. They gave a harsh but realistic update on the Omega variant. They reminded the group of the impact of the misinformation campaign many Republicans had been involved with. The details were difficult and when it ended, the room was very quiet.

The president thanked the team and Jim escorted them out. Next in were Homeland Security and the FBI. They provided an update on the terrorism threat level. They explained what was happening in the red zone counties and how local militia groups were, in many places, taking control of the region. The FBI spoke about very specific hot spots and how the local police had in those spots, for the most part, either disbanded or joined with the militia groups. They spoke about a possible strategy of using the National Guard to quell the militia but they assessed that it would likely spark a civil war in the targeted hot spots. The strategy, at present, was to observe and contain. They noted rising tension between red and green counties.

Again, the president thanked the team, and Jim ushered them out. He returned with the Joint Chief of Staff.

His update focused on operational logistics and the preparedness of the National Guard in terms of a containment role. He noted the challenges around county access and vaccines and test distribution. He detailed how many red zones, controlled by local militia, were blocking vaccines, test kits, and other aid targeted at the area. He reminded the group that the U.S. military had no authority to engage with American citizens. He echoed the concerns of the health team in regards to the constant campaign of misinformation and the association with widespread belief in certain regions that vaccines and tests were what were killing people.

The president thanked him and Jim walked him out and quickly returned.

"As you can see we have quite an issue. Aside from the Civil War, as a country, we've never faced anything like this. When we had enemies before, they were always outside our borders. This is a real test of the fabric of our country and our constitution. I've had Jim and a special team put together a plan. I'm asking him to run it by you folks and then, let's talk. Let's talk like one people, as our forefathers did," the president said.

The president waited for a moment before signaling to Jim to run through the plan. He wanted to gauge the expressions on the faces of those around him. More so, the expression of the GOP members. His team was on board, he knew that as he and Jim had hand-picked them. As he looked across the Republican faces, he caught a mix of concern and confusion.

"Jim, run us through the plan please," the president said.

Jim started up a presentation deck.

"First, I need to request that everything said in this room, stays in this room. What I'm going to present could be considered very controversial. Are we all in agreement?" Jim said.

Everyone in the room nodded and answered with a yes.

"Alright. I don't think anyone here would disagree with the science at this point. The Omega variant is a massive killer. However, as the medical health team outlined, it is significantly less so for those with the original two vaccines and the '22 and '24 boosters. There is a way out of this; it's vaccinations. Even for those without the boosters, as long as they have had the first two shots, this super booster can greatly reduce the deadliness of the variant. Early indications are that it can bring it down to approximately 3%. That is a number we can manage. 17% is not," Jim said.

He paused for a moment to let the information sink in.

"Alright, I can see that you all understand the need to get that 17% to 3% at worst. We have the super booster; we have enough of them but we face three major hurdles moving forward."

He paused once again, this time to take a drink of water.

"First, we need to correct the misinformation. What Trump did to this country was an absolute disgrace. I will say thank God he is gone from politics now but the damage he created is still here. We need to manage this situation with science and facts. To that point, this is what we plan to do. We will issue a law that censors all Covid, pandemic, or health information to all media outlets unless it is approved by our administration. We will temporarily suspend all social media platforms. We will establish a government site to provide accurate and up-to-date information. We will issue a bipartisan, unified message about the realities of what is happening and the scientific, medical facts of the

Omega variant. We will establish a daily plan and status update that will be led by members of both parties and the appropriate medical professionals."

Jim paused again, this time waiting for the tsunami. It wasn't long before it came.

"Jesus, this sounds a whole lot like bloody North Korea. How the hell do you expect us to get behind that?" Matt Cleff, the House Speaker, said.

"Hold on, Matt. I know it seems a little out there but we have a unique situation on our hands," the president replied, standing up and waving his hands for calm.

"Damn, Mike, a little out there is an understatement," Matt said.

"I know, Matt. Just hear the whole plan through and we can talk about it all," the president replied.

"All right. Jim, keep going," Matt said.

"The second challenge is acceptance. When the vaccine was first available, we had a good uptake. However, we eventually stalled around 65%. When the fifth wave hit in early 2022, we bumped up to close to 70% but that is still well short of the herd immunity number the medical and science team just told you about. Countries like Canada, New Zealand, and the United Kingdom managed to achieve adoption in the low 90% range and are not being impacted in the same way by this Omega in the way we are."

Jim took a pause, again letting the message set in.

"Acceptance is strongly tied to messaging. Even if we make inroads on the misinformation, an uptick in adoption may take time. We don't have the luxury of time right now."

Jim showed a series of pictures of bodies lying dead in houses and of mass burning of bodies in ditches.

"Jesus, this isn't what America should be," Republican Senator Clint Ray muttered.

"Clint, this is in your district," the president replied.

Clint went quiet as did the rest of the room.

"Look, I know, this has all caught us off guard. I think we got a little used to these occasional spikes. We'd lose a few people here or there but this is different. This one is devastating," Jim said.

All those around the table nodded; there was no other way to look at it.

"So, we need to get people vaccinated. We need to cull the deaths and regain some semblance of a proper medical system. Right now, hospitals in the red zones are completely overrun. To that end, we intend to make the super booster mandatory. We also intend to set up temporary health centers where those who are infected will be taken to. We need them out of the general public. There will be mandatory testing and those found positive will be moved to these facilities, by force if necessary," Jim said.

He stopped and stepped back a half step, almost as if expecting a foul wind.

"My God. You are talking about a totalitarian state. Mike, there is no way Americans are going to accept this. It goes completely against the constitution. Look, I get some of the thinking behind it, especially after the briefings but even if I agreed, I do not see any way to sell this to the people," the House Speaker said.

"Matt, I know. We are in a very challenging period in history. I've agonized over this for weeks. I see the numbers every day. We are losing millions, Matt, millions. This isn't about a gentle nudge to the left or the right. It's not even left or right anymore; it's about basic survival. We went from the leaders in finding a cure for this virus to the bottom of the barrel in vaccine rates. Why? because everyone has an agenda. Let's be honest here, you guys convinced a nation it was cheated after 2020 and forever put a stain on democracy, the very democracy we created, and for what, power and wealth? You all know it's true. We're behind closed doors. You kissed the ring of the man who created fake news and then assholes like Tucket made millions stoking it. You all supported that crap, hoping it would get you reelected. We were elected in the first place to represent our constituents. Do you really feel we are doing a good job?" the president asked loudly.

He stood up and walked around the Oval Room looking down at those seated.

"You are all fully vaccinated. I know you are; I'm the damn president and I've watched each of you GOP leaders downplay the dangers of the virus, support, indirectly and directly, anti-vaccination campaigns, and push for legislation against mask mandates. How's that working out now? The majority of red zones in America are in your jurisdiction. You heard the health update, 17%. How are the constituents in your districts doing? How about the ones that lost everything because you sold them lies? You had no problems selling lies, but you're not sure you can sell the reality that is happing in your states right now. Jim, show us the information on the deaths in each of our friend's districts please."

Jim made his way to the keyboard.

"Hold on, hold on. Mike, you know this is a whole lot more complicated than you make it out to be. We have a complex country and even more complex politics. We all know this isn't the country of our forefathers. It has changed and we are the party that has tried to preserve those values and our constitution while you cater to BLM and Antifa," Matt said.

The president sat back down. He hadn't lost his steam but he knew there was at least some truth in what Matt had said. The country, the world for that matter, was more complex.

"Matt, the question is how do we bridge our recent history? You heard the briefings; we are facing the greatest challenge in this country since the Civil War. Doing what we have been doing won't save this country," the president said.

Matt shifted a little in his chair. He looked across at his team and then back at the president. "I get the situation we're in. What I'm struggling with are the draconian actions I've heard so far. I'm not supportive of blowing up America to save her. That said, let's hear the rest of the plan."

The president looked at Jim and nodded.

"Alright, the final part is taking back the management of the transportation infrastructure in this country. As you heard in the briefing, militias control access in and out of as much as 20% of this country right now. We need to take that back in order to address the growing chaos and distribution of the super booster and medical help. To that end, we intend to enact a temporary bill to enable the military to take action on American soil and, if need be, against American citizens."

Jim paused at that point to allow the GOP members to absorb the last comment.

"The military will be deployed to take control of the militia groups and establish military controls on all transportation links. We intend to temporarily disarm these militias until the crisis passes," Jim said.

"Jesus, you can't be serious. That would drive a civil war, not to mention the issue with the Second Amendment," one of the GOP members exclaimed.

Matt calmed his team down. "Mike, Jim, I'm sure you can appreciate the enormity of the deviation from our traditional American life. Here is another issue. As your team pointed out, the majority of these regions are in Republican states. We follow this plan and we are done as a party. Yes, we have a unique crisis, a damn big one, but there is no way I support something that finishes off our relationship with our people. Jim, rightly or wrongly, we represent our constituents. They are different than yours are. We have two Americans now. Yours and ours. Which one are we fixing?" he said.

The president stood up to walk over to Matt. As he got near, Matt stood up and for a moment they stared each other down.

The president then smiled and extended his hand. "Matt, we go a long way back, me and you. You're partially right. We do have two segments of America now but we are all still under the stars and stripes. We have to save America, all of it, or we lose it all," the president said.

Matt nodded slightly. "Maybe, maybe your right, we all want to save America. We just have different views on how to do it," he said.

"Will you look at the proposal?" the president asked.

"Of course, we will. We know what's at stake. We will likely come back with a counter-proposal."

"You know that is exactly what we expected. Just be quick. You've seen the numbers."

They shook hands again. Jim escorted everyone out of the Oval Office and returned.

"Jim, what do you think?" the president asked as he slid down into his chair.

"Sir, if I were a betting man, I'd hold on to my money."

"Yes, I would too, Jim. Let's see what they come back with."

First Assignment

Will was over the moon when he got the call. He was assigned to unit R17. He and three others were to do the overnight shift, Tuesday through Saturday, on a major secondary road. Better yet, Carlos was on the same crew.

It seemed that for the secondary roads, the militia was assigning crews of four. The crews were a mix of either two veterans and two rookies or one veteran and three rookies, which was the case for Will and Carlos.

As usual, the two met at Bill's for a few afternoon beers. Even though the crowd was shrinking daily, the bar was upbeat. All five regulars from the bar had made the cut with the new militia and two of them, Will and Carlos, were making their debut that night. It was a reason to celebrate and Carlos was celebrating.

"Listen, Carlos, ya gotta watch how much beer you drink. We don't wanna show up drunk and all on the first night," Will said into Carlos' ear over the loud music.

Carlos turned and smiled back. "Yeah, I got that. We got time, Will. We'll enjoy some more and then drive up early so we can be ready," Carlos replied and grabbed Will around the shoulder.

Will smiled. Heck, that made sense, and yeah, they had earned it.

He raised his glass and let out a hoot to which the whole bar hooted back.

They did as they planned and when 9 pm rolled around, they hit the road. They decided to drive together, save on gas and all. The fact was, gas was getting harder to find and was a whole lot more expensive.

"Ya know, Will, I think this is pretty much the most exciting thing I ever done in my life," Carlos said as they drove the quiet Texas road.

"Me too. I always wanted to serve but I was never too healthy. Now I got a chance to do it the right way. Not for Washington but for Texas."

"Hell yeah, buddy," Carlos said and high-fived him.

Once again, Will smiled and then turned to look out the window, out across the darkening Texas night.

"Yo, Will, what ya think about having to pay for our uniforms?" Carlos asked.

"I'm okay with that, you know. They ain't got money from the government like the army does, so I guess it makes sense."

"Yeah, that does make sense, and heck, they look damn good."

Will grinned and looked down at his uniform. Never in a million years did he think he would get to wear such a uniform. They could have charged him $500; he would have found the money.

He looked out the window again, at this country, one he was now enlisted to protect.

About twenty minutes later they arrived at the new checkpoint. It was easy to see. The group had put together little sheds on each side of the room with a rudimentary barricade. The sheds also had a deck with a railing so the guards could look up and down the road. As they got closer to the checkpoint, they could see a rumble strip along the ground on the side of the road

"Shit, man, this is the real deal. We gonna control everything here. This is gonna be fun," Carlos said as he pulled over to the side.

As soon as they stopped the pickup, a spotlight was shone on the car and they were asked to identify themselves.

"We're with the R17 unit," Will yelled out.

The light went out and a man yelled over, "Good, come on over and meet the team."

Escape to the North

"Alright, we all here cause we gotta get out of this place. We know if we stay, we gonna die. It ain't gonna be easy. Lots of guys are trying, and cause we're in a red zone, they got us real locked down. We got a plan though. We got a good plan. We got Mickey here. He was sanitation for the New York subway. He knows bout old closed tunnels. Ones that can get us out of the Barrio," Big Al said.

Big Al looked over at Mickey.

Mickey pulled out a map from his backpack. He put it down on the table.

Jimmy looked down at it. The map was old, quite old.

"The subway here in New York is real fucking old. There are tunnels on tunnels. Some of them are forgotten but I know them. I know the ones that gonna get us out of this zone," Mickey said.

A few of the guys' high-fived Mickey.

"We gonna have to break through a couple of old wooden barriers and there's gonna be a mess of water and rats and shit. We also gonna have to walk a long way so you gonna need backpacks. We gonna arrange for some food and stuff to get us into a green zone. Once we get there, we should be able to resupply before we move on," Mickey said.

"Why don't we just stay there? We'll be in a green zone," someone asked.

"Cause we all registered as red zone residents and we missing the vaccine passport which is registered with the government. Their gonna find us if we try and stay there."

"I heard something about fake IDs. What about doing that once we're there?" another man asked.

"No. It ain't like a driver's license. That vaccine card has got some bio thing in it which ties it to the person. We looked into it a whole lot—can't be done, at least we can't. We gonna have to keep going once we get out of this zone. We got more plans once we come out of the tunnels. Leon has been working on that," Big Al said.

Mickey packed his map up and Leon laid his down.

"Now, I was a train engineer for years, running freights all around New York state and up by the Canadian border. I know the routes, the ones that can get up to a place where we can make a final run into Canada," Leon said.

Again, there was a level of excitement.

"That is the plan, guys. You'll know our target is Canada. They got things right up there. No red zones up there, no zone. Pretty much everyone is immune, and they are okay with folks like us coming in. We just got to get out of this goddam country," Big Al said.

"Canada is a long way," Jimmy replied.

"That's why we gonna get a ride," Big Al said.

"We gonna ride the rails like they did in the old days," Leon replied.

"What about county borders?" someone asked.

"The plan is to get to a yellow zone the first day and a green zone by day two. From there the routing for anything going to Canada follows all green counties. Once we get to a green zone, we're clear to the Canadian border," Leon said.

"So, how do we get into Canada?" Jimmy asked.

"That's Phil's job," Big Al replied.

Leon took his map away and Phil put one down. It was Lake Ontario.

"I used to run rescue operations out of Rochester. I know the lake; I know the typical security routes and the ones they avoid. When we get near the border, we're gonna get off the train and make our way down to an old rescue marina. It's technically shut down but I got two old buddies who are gonna pick us up in a rescue boat. We should have a clear passage into Canada under the guise of a rescue," Phil said.

Jimmy looked around the room. He was impressed; this crew had it together, far more than he had expected. He looked over at Big Al and gave him a little nod. Big Al nodded back.

"You guys got this thing laid out well, damn well. The question is, what do you need from me?" Jimmy asked.

Big Al looked over at a man who had been sitting in the dark in the corner the whole time. The man stood up and stepped into the light. Jimmy recognized him immediately. "Shit, man, you're DeSantos," he said.

"Damn right, I am." DeSantos grinned.

The Virus Spreads

The first thing Bobby did when he woke up the next morning was to check on Sarah. Once he did, he wasn't happy with what he saw.

"How are you feeling, kiddo?" Bobby asked.

"Not good, Daddy. I'm really hot and my head is spinning. I think I need some medicine," she replied.

Bobby put his hand on her head. It was so hot it almost burned his hand.

"Am I okay, Daddy?" she asked.

"Not too bad but yes, we'll need to get you some medicine, kiddo. Lucky, we got some stuff here," he replied and gave her a little hug.

He made his way to the kitchen and found his mother sitting there.

"Good morning, Mom," he said.

"You let your wife die. Are you going to do the same to your daughters?" she said.

He took an orange juice out of the fridge and sat down.

"What do you want me to do, Mom?"

"Save your daughters for Christ's sake. Sarah has Covid, we both know that. She needs help. If she stays, laying on that bed, we gonna be burying her alongside your father, in that dirty old mud. Your father belongs there, she doesn't."

"Alright, ya, she got Covid, I know. How do you think I feel? Goddam horrible if you really want to know. I loved Lilly, I love my girls and, right now, I fucking hate Dad," he screamed.

"You should. He controlled you and your brother. He made your decisions for you and you just went along."

"He was our father; we trusted him. Why wouldn't we?"

His mother sighed and took a drink of her coffee. She looked up and said, "Because he was not a good man."

Bobby got up and walked around the kitchen. A piece of him already knew what his mother had said was true. If he was fair to himself and his memories, he would have hated his father years ago but no kid wanted that, so he made those slight adjustments, over time, to those memories.

"What can I do with Sarah? There is no room at the hospital. We can't even see a doctor," Bobby said.

"Here, yes, but the situation is much better in green zones. You need to get your daughters to a green zone."

He sat back down again. "It's not quite so easy," he replied.

"If you want to be a good father, you will find a way," she said, got up, and left the kitchen.

He thought about what she had said. She was right. He could hear Sarah coughing in the background. It was a hard reminder of Lilly.

As he struggled There was one person he could go to. He preferred not to, but his options were limited. He picked up his phone and dialed a number. "Jerome, it's Bobby. I need to talk to you about something."

The GOP Response

"Sir, we have word back from the GOP team. They want to meet again, today," Jim said.

The president looked up at Jom.

"Alright, let's get it done. Get the briefing together for 4 pm this afternoon and inform the GOP team to be here in the Oval Room for the same time."

"Yes, sir."

"Jim, we gotta close this thing today."

"Yes, sir. We do," Jim said and quickly left the room.

The president looked back down at his daily briefing. The numbers were accelerating. Cases in the red and yellow zones, where testing was still present, were at record levels. The more concerning number was the deaths; they were tracking to that forecast line, unfortunately.

He spent the day going through his meetings as planned but his head, his thoughts, were about what was to happen later in the day.

Come 3:30 pm, the president was at his desk, preparing. He understood the importance of the coming meeting. It was not only the biggest of his life, it might well be among the biggest in the history of an American president.

At 4 pm on the nose, there was a knock on the door.

"Come in, Jim," the president said.

The door opened and a procession worked its way into the room.

"Matt, I appreciate you and your team addressing this in such short order," the president said.

"Mike, we know this is a crisis," Matt replied.

"Folks, please, take a seat," Jim said.

The president waited for everyone to be comfortably settled in before he stood.

"First, I want to thank you all for your focus on this. Second, don't take this the wrong way, but this is a no-bullshit session. I know we have said that in the past, but I honestly sense this crisis is different," the president said.

"Every crisis has its own particular structure. This one is exceptional. We had our internal debrief after our last meeting. We know there is a shortage of time in front of us so we are here to also find a no-bullshit solution, as you put it," Matt said.

"To that end, let's start with the GOP's feedback. Matt, the floor is yours," the president said.

Matt took the floor and walked through the GOP's assessment of the three strategic briefings they had been given a couple of days earlier.

For the most part, the GOP's assessment was in line with the administration. There was some disagreement on the level of control the local militias had in various states. There was also a comment about the difference in messaging since the election which led to a short debate on muzzling Trump. The party was finally moving away from him.

Once the assessment was done, the president called for a break and Jim had snacks brought in. The president wanted an integrated working group and he knew a little casual time was helpful.

"Thanks again to you and your team for making this a priority," the president said as he pulled up a chair beside Matt.

"Mike, we have a real problem on our hands. This is everyone's priority," Matt replied.

"We do. Matt, we have to find a unified solution to this."

"We do, but we are coming at it from different places. Our bases are very different, possibly more so than any other time in the past two hundred years. You were right, you know, last time when you said we are elected to represent our constituents. We have to keep that in consideration with what we are supporting."

The president nodded. The statement was true for him as well. The challenge, if it could be called that, was how valuable the needs of constituents are when they are based on misinformation or flat-out ignorance. He knew Matt and his team had a much bigger challenge on that front than he did.

"We do have very different bases, Matt. Come on, let's get this thing moving," the president said and patted Matt on the shoulder.

"Jim, let's get back to it," the president said.

The food was cleared away and people retook their seats.

"Matt, the floor is yours again," the president said.

"Thank you, Mike. Alright, we are on some common ground here in terms of the situation. What we differ on is the approach. Now I know this isn't what you all here were hoping to hear but we face a different challenge. Our base, especially in the south, is ripe with misinformation. Yes, I know where it came from but the challenge is changing the mindset that permeates these regions. We agree with the premise of the first point in your approach. The misinformation, especially those targeted at the virus and vaccination, needs to be shut down."

Matt stopped for a moment. "Why do I feel as if I'm hearing a 'but'?" the president said.

"Because there is one. We won't support shutting down media; it goes against the premise of the first amendment of the constitution. What we do support is a fine-based system, with increasing fines for anything that is defined as misinformation based on a non-partisan panel. We also agree to hold daily joint briefings targeted at providing accurate information. We agree to shut down the known groups on social media but that goes both ways, far left and far right."

The president glanced momentarily over at Jim who nodded. There was a reason why Jim was his VP.

"We're good with the balance on the left and right groups. I'd like to see the proposals on the penalties. They need to have teeth if this is going to work. I'm sure we can work out a sensible daily plan. Let's move to the next point," he said.

"On the vaccination front, we are prepared to announce that all the Republican house and senate members are fully vaccinated. We do not support mandatory vaccinations; it goes against the party's principle on freedom of rights. What we suggest is a program run by the local state which provides significant financial rewards for reaching immune status. It would be supported by mobile vaccination and testing units operated by local groups."

Matt paused to read the room. There were no immediate replies, so he continued.

"We will support the establishment of emergency military Covid hospitals to be set up in all red zones but not mandatory stays. We believe that based on recent feedback, the majority of those sick in the red zones will be willing to attend a medical facility. The nightly burning of bodies in those areas has had a terrifying effect on people. We believe that once in the facility, they will stay until they recover or otherwise."

The president looked over at Jim again. It took a moment this time but Jim nodded again.

"I think we can work with this however I am concerned about local support. It is critical for getting buy-in. We need the local government structure to work step in step with the feds. We both know that the federal government is a negative in those areas," the president said.

"We've been in touch with the state and local Republicans in all red zones. We have commitments from all of them. The new messaging will help with acceptance as well."

The president nodded. "You have the floor again," he said.

"On the third point, access control. We agree that access is critical to support the vaccine role and the medical facilities. I don't want to play politics here but the zoning control executive order is what laid the groundwork for the challenges we have today. We are dead set against supporting homeland enablement of the military. We will support a special deployment of the National Guard and agree to take them from green zones with a balanced mix from Democratic and Republican regions. We see them set up posts alongside the spots where militias have taken control and work with them to jointly manage access in and out. We will absolutely not support any plan that takes guns away from people. This is our reply to your proposal. We will send a written summary after the session is done."

Matt sat down. He was exhausted, mentally. While the details of what he presented might have seemed scant, he had been working for the better part of forty-eight hours. It had been meeting after meeting, call after call, all working to get a party—which had been massively split for the last eight years—on the same page. The president knew Matt well. They had grown up, so to speak, in the system together. Matt knew what could sell and what could not. He had crafted the best possible response he could, one that threaded the needle between GOP values, his base, and appeasing the Democratic president.

As the president thought about the counter-proposal, he knew he might be able to make it work on the first two items but the third one was going to be an issue.

The president did not need to look at Jim. He knew there was to be no nod this time. There wasn't.

"Matt and all of you, I appreciate how much work went into this. Hell, we've been at this long enough to know how hard it is to get a simple majority on small bills. I know what you've done in the background. That said, on the surface, we cannot agree with item number three. We will take it away and get back to you," the president said.

The GOP team all stood up and one by one they shook the president's hand. They all knew, left and right, that they were closer as a group than they had been for more than a decade. The question was whether or not it was going to be enough.

The Plan is in Play

"Damn, I figured there must be someone big behind this thing. You a legend, man," Jimmy said.

DeSantos looked at Jimmy, sizing him up as he likely did to everyone he met. After a very long couple of seconds, DeSantos smiled.

"You're right, I am legend and this legend knows when it's time to move on."

Jimmy shook DeSantos' hand.

"Speaking of time to move on, we make our first move tomorrow night, midnight. We will meet here and head over to the first tunnel entrance. Now, we gonna need $500 from each of you to cover various costs that we got. We will need the money when we meet here tomorrow. Also, we got a list of things you gonna need to bring for the trip. You gonna need water, food, and warm clothes. It's gonna take about three days to get to Canada," Big Al said.

$500, Jimmy thought. He figured this thing might just be too good to be true. $500 might as well be $5 million. He didn't have either.

Big Al put his hand on Jimmy's back. "Everything okay, bro?" he asked.

"Yeah, yeah, I'm good. Hey, I'll see you tomorrow."

Jimmy shook hands and hugged it out with the group of guys that were there. He counted ten in total including himself. He wondered how many would be back the next day.

He made his way back out to the street. The scene had become harsher. It seemed that the power was out in many places and darkness had enveloped the large parts of the city. It should have been his world, the gangster world they talked about so many nights over booze and blow. Somehow, the reality of it was so far from the vision. It was death, darkness, and a lack of humanity that stunned even the hardest gangbanger. While it was the world they thought they longed for, Jimmy and many others wanted nothing more than to leave.

He wended his way home, avoiding his usual corners. Once he reached his place, he sat down on the couch and pulled out his phone. He made a list of those who owed him money. The list added up to over a grand, but he knew better. Most of the guys were deadbeats. He'd be lucky to collect $500.

He grabbed a beer out of the fridge and headed back to the couch. He took a deep, long draw from the beer and started to make his calls. As expected, most of the guys declined the call but he did get through to a few guys. He had commitments for about $280.

He hung the phone up and went into the bedroom. He pulled the bottom drawer out of his dresser and turned it over. Underneath there was an envelope taped to the bottom. Jimmy ripped the envelope open. Inside was $230, his emergency fund or at least what was left of it.

He tucked it into his pocket with the twenty-odd dollars that were in there all ready and headed out to grab the supplies. $250, he needed to be thrifty.

A half-hour later, he was back home with $202 left to his name. He knew he had his work cut out the next day. He grabbed the last beer in the fridge, downed it in the kitchen, and headed to bed.

One Final Counter

"Mr. President, the team has finished with the analysis of the GOP counter and has a series of recommendations," Jim said.

The president sat pensively for a moment and then said, "Alright, send them in Jim."

Jim walked to the door and led the group in.

"First I want to thank you all for the work you've done over the last week. This is a unique time in American history. We have to make this work, we truly do," the president said very emotionally.

"Well, sir, in terms of the three pillars, we believe we can find common ground on the first two. The GOP suggestions and the thinking behind them are reasonably sensible given the Republican base. Where we are stuck potentially is on the third pillar. The GOP is not ready to go head-to-head with the more militant portion of the base. There are reasons for that. They cannot be seen taking the siding with the government against what much of the base sees as their freedom fighters. Their base may not all want to take up arms but many of them support what the militias are doing. It would be suicide for their party," General Anderson said.

"So, what are you thinking, General?" the president asked.

"They will never support an executive order on the military so our best bet is a hand-picked National Guard unit from green zone. We would work with the Republicans to establish a relationship with the various militias. We would work outstanding protocols for managing movements."

The president looked over at Jim. "Thoughts, Jim?"

"It may facilitate movement, perhaps enough to get the vaccines moving and establish the medical facilities but we would not be in control. We would be at the whim of the militias and more so the Republicans who would hold the relationships with them. The most dangerous part of the counter is the fact that the militias would not be disarmed. As you know, sir, there are a lot of guns out there. These militias are better armed than the National Guard."

"Praise the Second Amendment," the president said sarcastically.

"I somehow doubt the founding fathers had AR-15s in mind when they wrote the amendment," Jim replied.

"You and I both, Jim. Now, what do we counter with on this third pillar?"

"We need control, sir. We don't deal with this variant without unfettered access across the country. We need to press for the dismantling of all militia control points and the establishment of green zone National Guards, non-local guards staffed control points. We also need to ensure the militias do not establish a subsequent control point further inside the region. That is why disarming them is the preferred route. All that said, my belief is the GOP will never support any form of disarming," Jim replied and strategically paused.

"Our counter should be the following. First, the militia control points are taken down, and the National Guard are established as the only access control around all red zones. Second, we, jointly with GOP representation, get a handle on the militia membership. If we can't disarm them, we need to know what and who we are dealing with. Third, we need meetings with the heads of the key militias on the large red zones. We need to craft a written agreement stipulating they will not interfere with the vaccine rollouts or the setup and operations of the medical facilities. In exchange, we will allow them to share the security work involved in the vaccines and equipment rollout and the ongoing security of the facilities. This throws them a bone and some income. It would also allow us the ability to monitor the militias."

The president looked at Jim closely. He was analyzing the feedback. It was consistent with the conversations they had had over the past twenty-four hours and mainly in line with the president's view. He personally wanted at least a partial disarming of the militias, removing the military-grade equipment, in the event that a battle breaks out. He knew overwhelming firepower would end any potential conflict quickly. He wanted the U.S. armed forces to have that overwhelming power. He was very concerned about the balance of power between the well-armed militias and National Guard, who were not quite the American military.

"Do any of you think we can push the envelope any further? Perhaps the removal of military grade weapons," the president asked.

Everyone in the room looked around at each other. The Joint Chiefs of Staff looked at the president and said, "Given a longer window of time, yes. Under the current situation, no. Sir, I would advise that we prepare an executive order to mobilize the military if the plan fails. We have established a red zone mobilization plan and will have it on standby."

The president nodded. That was the backup plan. He knew it would be effective but would equally tear the country apart. He knew the military executive order would be challenged in the courts but, by the time it was heard, he hoped any questions around it would have already been answered.

He was facing two equally drastic options. Break the country with military action or allow the country to break itself by ignorance and false bravado.

"Jim, that's our responsibility and let's get that executive order together as a backup. Mark, I want a full review of the military contingency first thing tomorrow morning," the president said and then waved everyone out of the room.

Finding a Way

"We need some help, Jerome. You know Lilly passed, well my dad just passed too," Bobby said.

"Shit, Bobby, I'm really sorry to hear that. It's a bad time out there right now," Jerome replied.

"Worse, Sarah is sick now and the hospitals here are closed down cause of how many other people are sick."

"You are a red zone, right?"

"Yeah, that's the problem. I need help getting into the Houston area. I hear there are some green parts there. I need to get her to a hospital. I know you got that boat; I figured maybe if we could get down to the Gulf, you could get us there cross the water."

There was a momentary silence.

"I dunno, Bobby. They got some pretty big fines for people doing stuff like that and they got militia groups out there now too. Maybe we could get her into a hospital down here. We're a yellow zone now so it's not as bad as where you are."

"Maybe, honestly I'm good with any hospital at this point. How about this, Jerome? We get her down there and if we can get into a good hospital, alright. If not, then you take us to Houston."

"Hmmm, ya, alright. I guess we can do that. Your biggest challenge is gonna be getting out of your zone from what I hear," Jerome said.

"Thanks. Let me figure out how and when we are going to do this and I'll get back to you," Bobby replied and hung up.

"Who was that, Daddy?" Sasha asked.

Bobby turned to see her standing in the doorway.

"That was Uncle Jerome, over in Port Arthur."

Sasha looked closely at her father.

"What were you talking about?" she asked inquisitively.

"Well, he was wondering when we would like to visit him."

Sasha ran over to Bobby and hugged him. "Daddy, I would love that. Uncle Jerome has the best house and he has a super-fast boat too."

"His place is pretty cool and he does love having you guys there."

Sasha's smile faded. "But, Daddy, I don't think they are in a red zone are they? How would we get there?"

Bobby held Sasha's face with his hands on either side and said, "I'll take care of that, my little doll."

Bobby kissed her on the forehead. She smiled, said, "You better, Daddy," and skipped out of the room.

Bobby waited a few moments and took his laptop back out. He opened up the maps to the local waterways that led to the Gulf and started to make a plan, one which he hoped would allow him to right some of the wrongs he now realized he had been responsible for.

Losing the Battle

"Mr. President, I just received word from the GOP that they are not going to support our proposed changes to the third leg of the plan. It seems that we will not be unified in this battle," Jim said.

The president sighed and sat down.

"Jim, I'm not surprised. The truth is that America hasn't been a unified country for a long time. We were when we had a purpose. We stood together when we were a beacon for what was right in this world," the president said.

He paused for a moment, collecting his thoughts and, a little bit, his emotions.

"It's funny, in many ways, we, as a country, are at our best when we have an enemy, something we can unify against. It's how this country started, battling the British. WWII was our shining moment. We stood against the tyranny and evil of Nazi Germany and, despite the odds, we won. The Cold War was in some ways perfect for us. The Russians played their role as the enemy well. Since then the world has changed. The enemy is not so clear-cut. It isn't borders and uniforms, it's theology. It's harder for people to get their heads around it and a damn lot harder to root out."

He stood up and walked over to the Oval Office window.

"Now this, this bloody virus. Jesus, Jim, with the smallest of enemies, we're losing this goddam war. We're losing because of ourselves. I'd rather not be remembered as the president who lost America," he said very emotionally.

"Mr. President, we will do everything we can to ensure that doesn't happen," Jim replied.

The president looked at Jim quietly for a moment. "While I appreciate that, I'm not sure there is much we can do at this point. Be honest with me, Jim. We've been together a long time. I need your opinion on this. Are we going to win this war?"

"Sir, speaking with all due respect, the deck is stacked against us. You're right, historically we are at our best when promoting the democracy that we created. The real problem is that we don't even abide by what we are trying to sell around the world. The world has changed, technology has lifted the veil of propaganda. If we're honest with each other, propaganda is part of what we exported and helped made us great. You're right, when we had clear enemies, we could market our message with ease. Then, it was news. Today, it's messaging and for many reasons, half of America doesn't believe it, despite the serious impact of disbelief. Fake news and political extremeness have already destroyed this country," Jim replied.

The president turned and looked at him. He came and sat back down at his desk.

"So what the hell do we do?" he asked.

"We need to consider a plan B."

A Time for Rationing

Will headed out for some groceries ahead of another night of duty and found himself driving from grocery store to grocery store, only to find closed signs and 'out of supplies' on all of them.

"What the hell?" he mumbled to himself.

He decided to head over to Costco. If anything was going to have stuff, it was going to be Costco, he figured.

As he pulled in, he was relieved to see a relatively full parking lot.

He parked and headed toward the entrance. As he approached it, he could see something was going on.

When he got there, he found a group of people yelling and shoving at the door.

"What the hell is going on?" Will asked the crowd.

"They ain't letting no one in without a mask on," a young man replied.

"That ain't right. This is America," Will said.

He started to push his way forward. He was in uniform and most in the crowd let him through. He reached the front in a mood of bravado.

"Who's in charge here?" he asked.

"I am," a large black man in a security uniform said.

"You know you can't block us from coming in."

"Yeah, I can. It's because of you fucks that everybody's getting sick. Management says you can't come in without a mask on, so you ain't coming in."

Will turned and looked at the crowd behind him. He realized at that moment he was representing the entire group. He was, in effect, the man. The problem was, he wasn't used to being the man, despite how much he dreamed of it.

Unsure what to do, he turned back and attempted to push his way past the security guard. The guard, twice his size, grabbed Will and easily threw him to the ground. He found himself stunned. He was stunned from the impact of the ground but equally from the sheer violence of the incident. He was a small man and had managed to avoid conflict his whole life. The intensity of the moment caught him completely off guard.

As he struggle to right himself, the crowd drove forward past him and engaged with the security.

Hurt and embarrassed, Will scattered to the side and collected himself. Once he did, he slowly exited the battle scene. The physical pain was one thing, the emotional pain brought back deeply buried memories he wasn't ready to deal with.

He got up and headed back to his pickup. When he got there, he slowly took out his AR-15.

He walked back to what had become a full-on brawl and systematically sought out the security guard. He found him holding the doorway. Will raised the gun, looked him straight in the eye, and with a slight grin, pulled the trigger.

Packing Up

Jimmy spent the morning hunting people down. Specifically, hunting down those who owed him money. In the end, he had $573 in his pocket and a few bruised knuckles to go along with it.

He made his way back to his apartment. Along the way, he couldn't help but notice the stench of death. He had no doubt that each of the buildings he passed contained their share of rotting bodies. The death trucks had stopped coming by. The dead, at least in Jimmy's neighborhood, lay where they had died. His building was no exception. He had been smelling it for days.

When he arrived home, he headed to his bedroom, He took out his old backpack, the one he'd had since high school. It wasn't very big but it didn't matter; he didn't have much.

As he packed his few things into his bag, he thought about his life for a moment. So few things to represent it. He knew somewhere he had gone wrong. He also thought about his sister. Her life had gone right. She had always told him he needed to change. He figured one day he would. He just never knew when that day was. Now, it seemed to him, the day had passed.

He knew he owed his sister a call. She had left multiple messages. He wasn't ready for that conversation. Once he was in Canada, he'd make that call and patch things up, he figured.

He packed the last of the things he planned to bring. He then put two photos in his bag. The one family portrait they had done right after high school, and one of his mother.

As he put the pictures in his bag, he paused for a moment. He felt a wave of emotion. What the hell was going on in the world? he thought. Was this God's way of cleansing humanity? He had never believed in God or religion but there was something that felt biblical in what was happening.

He shook the thought off and headed to the kitchen. He opened the fridge and grabbed one of the two remaining beers. He then flopped down on the couch and turned on the TV. He had some time to kill before the meet-up. He found a movie on Netflix, Demons: Judgment Day. It seemed to fit the bill for where his life was at the moment.

Planning a Way Out

Bobby sat at the kitchen table looking through online maps on his laptop.

"So, have you made the right decision?" his mother asked as she came into the kitchen.

"Yes, I guess so. I've talked to Jerome about getting us to Houston and a green zone," he replied.

"About time," she said and left the kitchen.

Bobby turned back to the maps. He knew it was going to be tough to get out of the region. The main roads had been blocked for a while. The latest news was that the rural roads were also being blocked, both from outside and from inside. Militia groups were apparently blocking people from getting in or out of red zones and, more so, the government from entering the area. Getting out, for Bobby and his girls, was going to take some creativity.

He focused on the waterways. There were lots of rivers throughout the area. His plan, or at least the one that was evolving, was to head south of the city limits to Palmetto State Park and take the river down to Little White Lake. There, he could have Jerome pick him up in the boat. He would use GPS coordinates to arrange the meet. The danger would be when they crossed into the Terrebonne County as it was a yellow zone. He planned to flow downstream in a canoe disguised as a large log.

It made sense to crossover the county birder inland, as opposed to having Jerome run the risk of riding his boat into a red zone. He figured the yellow zone would likely be less patrolled.

He heard a loud and deep cough from Sarah's bedroom. He closed the laptop and rushed to her room.

Back on Duty

Will arrived at Bill's Bar and Grill late in the afternoon. He found Carlos sitting up at the bar.

"Yo, Will, what's happening?" Carlos yelled across the bar.

Will quietly walked over to Carlos. They exchanged handshakes and chest pumps. As usual, Carlos almost knocked Will over.

They both sat down at the bar. Carlos waved the bartender over.

"Get my friend here a cold beer," he said to the young man.

"You got it."

"You ready for tonight?" Carlos asked.

"Yeah, sure, of course," Will replied a little cautiously.

Carlos turned and looked at him. "You alright, buddy?" he asked.

Will squirmed for a moment. He was hoping his discomfort wouldn't show but he had never been good at hiding his emotions.

"Yeah, just feeling a little off. Didn't sleep well last night is all."

"Hey buddy, shit happens. Let's get a few beers in you. That will make you feel better," Carlos said and patted Will on the back.

The beer arrived and Will quickly put it down.

"Hey, man, you're thirsty tonight," Carlos said laughing.

"I guess I am," Will replied trying to smile.

The two of them spent a couple of hours drinking beer and talking shit. By the end of it, Will felt a whole lot better.

"Come on, Will, we gotta get on duty," Carlos said.

The two paid up and started to leave. As they did, Will glanced up at the TV. The news was on and the caption said, "Man wanted in shooting at Costco."

"Shit," he muttered and followed Carlos out the door.

An Unusual Adventure

"Where are we going, Daddy?" Sasha asked as they drove in the middle of the night, pulling a canoe on their trailer.

"I thought we would have a little adventure," Bobby replied.

Sasha looked at Sarah. "Daddy, I don't know if it's a good time for an adventure for Sarah."

Bobby kept driving. He knew Sasha was right. What kind of parent would drag a sick kid out in the middle of the night on an adventure? He had thought about telling the girls during the day but worried that they would freak out or ask too many questions. Now, he was in a spot; he needed to come clean.

"Sasha, you know Sarah is sick, really sick. She has what Mommy and Grandpa had," Bobby said.

"I know, Daddy. She has Covid. How come we never got the vaccines?"

Bobby squirmed in his seat. The question was haunting him. In reality, it was the decision that was haunting him. If he could turn the clocks back, just once, he would do things differently.

"Honestly, Sasha, Daddy made a mistake. We should have gotten them."

"If we did, Daddy, Mommy would still be here, right?"

The comment hit Bobby hard. It did because he had begun to realize the truth in it. He had failed to listen to reason. Instead, he listened to the voice of hate and ignorance and paid a huge price. He increasingly hated his father and all those who ignorantly promoted falsehoods in the name of political alignment. He had been stupid to follow such ignorance when inside himself, he knew better.

"Yes, she probably would be."

Sasha was quiet again, looking out of the window as they drove along a small rural road.

"What we are doing tonight Sasha is saving Sarah," he said.

She smiled. "I know."

They drove on for some time down the 330 and, in the middle of a dark stretch, Bobby pulled off the road, pulled into the tall grass, and turned the lights off.

"This is where we are going to have a little canoe ride," Bobby said.

He turned the car off and got out. Sasha also got out of the car.

"Come on Sasha, let's get our adventure started."

Together, Bobby and Sasha removed the canoe from the trailer and placed it in the Vermilion River against the shore.

"Sasha, we need to grab some long grass and branches. The plan is to make this look like a floating log," Bobby said as he scouted through the vegetation.

"Why would we do that, Daddy?"

Bobby stopped what he was doing and kneeled beside her. "Sasha, we need to be very quiet and careful about leaving this area. People in other areas, places that don't have as many sick, don't want us coming in but that is where we need to bring Sarah."

Sasha looked at Bobby and smiled. "Then we will be very quiet, Daddy."

The two of them quietly finished setting up the canoe. Once they were done, Bobby carefully lifted Sarah out of the car and placed her on the floor in the canoe. He had already put padding and blankets in it earlier in the day.

"Now, Sasha, you keep an eye on the canoe while I hide the car." She nodded supportively and held tight onto the canoe.

Bobby got back into the car and drove it, lights off, along the shoreline until it was in a relatively thick batch of vegetation. He got out and lay some large branches across the car and trailer until it was nearly impossible to see.

He walked back to the canoe and hugged Sasha.

"Ready?" he asked.

"I am, Daddy."

The two climbed into the canoe. Bobby pushed them away from the shore. They pulled branches over them, lay back in the canoe, and let the current take them into the greatest adventure of their life.

Facing the Music

Will parked the pickup in the usual spot. He and Carlos double-timed it over to the gate as they were a few minutes late.

"What the hell, guys. You're late again. We're gonna have to put you on support duty if this keeps up," the militia lead yelled at them.

"Sorry, sorry we had a little issue getting going today," Carlos replied.

"Funny how that is becoming the daily norm for you two clowns. Shape up or you're off of line duty. You got that?"

"Yes, we got it," Will replied sheepishly.

The militia lead stormed off.

Will and Carlos climbed the ladder up to the guardhouse deck and relieved the other two guards.

"Shit, Will, we're gonna have to make sure we're on time going forward."

Will didn't respond; he walked over to the railing and quietly looked out over the horizon. Carlos walked over and stood beside him.

"Geez, Will, what's going on with you?"

Will continued to scan the horizon for a moment. He then turned to Carlos with a serious look on his face.

"Carlos, I did something bad."

"Will, we all do something bad sometimes," Carlos replied with a slight grin.

Will stared into Carlos' eyes. "I did something real bad," he said emotionally.

Carlos quickly changed his attitude. "Will, what did you do?"

"I shot someone."

Carlos looked surprised. "What do you mean shot someone?"

"I shot a security guard at Costco yesterday."

Carlos spun around to Will. "Shit, Will, I saw that in the news. You shot that security guard."

Hearing Carlos speak those words seemed to spur Will on somehow.

"Yeah, I shot him. He attacked me."

Carlos said nothing at first. Will also remained quiet, waiting for some form of response.

"Well, if he attacked you then maybe it's okay," Carlos finally said.

"Yes, it was self-defense."

"Yeah, self-defense. You need to be able to defend yourself."

"I do and I did," Will said, almost proudly.

Carlos smiled at Will. The smile then faded. "I think you're gonna have to tell someone about this."

Will quietly walked back and forth in front of Carlos.

"I dunno, I guess maybe," he replied.

"Well, it was on the news and there is a video. I think it's probably better that you tell someone rather than they come and get you."

Will hemmed and hawed a little and then said, "I think you're right, Carlos. Maybe after the shift today we could talk to the lead. I'm sure he will know what I should do."

"Yeah, that's a good idea. I bet he'll know exactly what to do," Carlos confidently replied.

Will looked out over the dark road they were guarding and wondered if perhaps he would find himself on the other side of a guarded wall.

The Great Escape

Jimmy showed up at the bar around 11:40 pm.

"Yo, Jimmy, glad you made it, brother," Big Al said seeing Jimmy walk in.

"Hey, wouldn't miss it for the world."

Big Al pulled Jimmy closer. "You got the entry fee, right?"

"Yeah, I'm good, brother."

Big Al smiled and patted him on the chest. "Shit, that's great. I wanted you with us," he said.

Jimmy looked around the bar. He recognized many faces from the meeting. "So, what's next?" he asked a little nervously.

"We wait for DeSantos. He should be here soon. Hey, have a beer, it's on me."

"For sure. Thanks, brother."

Jimmy sat back and looked around the bar. It truly was a dive but for many people, like Jimmy, that wasn't a bad thing. He knew the rich in Manhattan enjoyed their hoity toiti, high-end restaurants. In Jimmy's mind, that was about how much you could spend, publicly that was. It was a competition. It was who had the biggest dick when, at the end of the day, none of them did. They would happily throw each other under the bus to gain an inch.

No, the people in his dive had little themselves but at least they were real. It wasn't a competition, it was community and survival, together. Despite the struggle at times, he much preferred his world.

Jimmy finished his beer just as DeSantos walked in. He gestured to Big Al, Jimmy, and several others to follow him. There were ten of them at this point, it seemed everyone was able to ante up.

They all got up and followed him to the back of the bar. He opened a door and they all quickly rushed in.

"Sit down," DeSantos said loudly.

They all quickly sat down.

"First, we ante up. No one goes anywhere with the payment," he said.

Everyone took out their money and put it on the table.

DeSantos counted each pile and put the money in a pocket on his backpack. He then took out a bunch of plastic bags and duct tape.

"Put these around your shoes and tape 'em up tight. Where we're going, you're gonna want to have these on," he said.

Everyone took two bags and taped them tight. Once they were done, they all stood up.

DeSantos smiled and smacked his hands together. "Shit ya, now we're ready for some adventure."

He took a gun out of his bag and checked the clip. He then put it into the back of his pants.

"Lead on, Mickey," DeSantos said.

Mickey headed out the door to the side room and across the bar. Everyone quietly followed. They reached the front door and Mickey paused. He opened the door and looked both ways.

He looked back at the group and said, "Not worried about the cops. I don't want no stragglers. Nobody is getting a free ride."

He stepped outside and started a brisk walk down the street. Everyone followed.

They covered about three blocks quickly and then ducked into a side door of a subway station. They made their way to a locked door. Mickey took out a set of keys and open the door. Inside they headed down a long set of stairs to a large opening and stopped.

"This is one of the old platforms. It ain't been used for a real long time. At the back end of the platform, there is a service tunnel to one of the old lines. One that gets us off the island," Mickey said.

He began to walk quickly again. Everyone followed.

They reached the end of the platform. Mickey took a crowbar out of his backpack and pried a door open. As soon as it opened, the stench poured out.

"Holy shit, what died in there?" Big Al asked.

"Sewage," Mickey grinned.

"I see why we need the bags," Jimmy said.

One by one, the ten of them stepped through the doorway down a couple of steps into a murky, smelly liquid.

Mickey and DeSantos turned on flashlights and the walk began.

"Boys, this tunnel gonna take us across Harlem and down under the river to Randall's Island. From there we gonna walk the train line through the Bronx to West Chester. The Bronx is a yellow zone so we still gotta be careful when we come out of the tunnel. It's about five miles to the Bronx; we'll do another update then. We ain't gonna be moving too quickly through this tunnel so I figure about two hours to the Bronx."

The group started sloshing through the muck. Less than fifty meters into the tunnel, they found the rats. The flashlights showed them out. They scattered as the light hit them.

"God damn, I hate rats," one of the guys behind Jimmy said.

"Don't worry, they don't like us too much neither. They'll keep their distance," Mickey said.

The group trudged on quietly following the light that shone their way. Despite the plastic bags, Jimmy's feet eventually became soaked. He ripped the bags off as a couple of other guys did.

The Omega Variant

About two hours later, they came to the end of the tunnel. Once again, Mickey took the crowbar out and pried the door at the end of the tunnel open.

"Alright boys, we gonna go up some stairs to a service building. It should be abandoned but we gotta be quiet, just in case," Mickey said.

DeSantos took his gun out of his pants. Mickey and DeSantos led the way up the stairs. They reached the top and Mickey took a set of keys out of his bag and unlocked the door. He turned to the rest of the guys and waved his hand, indicating to them to be quiet.

DeSantos opened the door slightly and looked out. He waved to the group to follow him and stepped out the door. Everyone followed him through the door. They stepped into a small, old service building. They walked to the exit door. Mickey took the crowbar out again and pried it open. He peered out and then looked back. "We're good," he said.

They all stepped out. Jimmy looked around; it was dark and quiet, just as he hoped it would be.

"Alright, you mugs, we got some walking to do now. We gonna need to cover about six more miles to our safe house for the day. We might be in a yellow zone now but we ain't got the paperwork to be here. If any of you get caught, you're on your own. So spread out and stay low. We don't want to be seen as a group. I'll lead the way and will wait at a spot I've picked out for this. We gonna stick to the tracks. Let's go," DeSantos said.

One by one, pausing to put distance between them, each member of the group got moving and quietly began walking the tracks.

As Jimmy got up onto the tracks, he looked back at Barrio, the place he had spent the bulk of his life. He knew it would never be what it had been but somehow at that point, it didn't much matter, he was still going to miss it.

Plan B

Jim escorted the last of the Plan B team into the Oval Office. Everyone found a seat.

The president stood up and walked around to the front of his desk. He sat down on the desk, an unusual act for him.

"Folks, this is incredibly difficult to say, but I think we are coming to the sad realization that we will not be able to save the entire country, not now at least. We need to implement plan B for the time being and look to reunify the country at some point going forward," the president said.

There was an uncomfortable silence across the group. They were all Washington veterans, many also veterans of the various American military events. They all bled red, white, and blue from their veins.

"I supposed we were not able to find common ground with the GOP," the House Minority lead said.

"Unfortunately, no."

"Sir, I suggest we go through the assessment one more time. I know we have all seen it individually but, for the sake of the country, I think we owe one last review, together," Jim said.

"That is exactly what we were planning. Bring in our presenters, Jim."

Jim walked to a side door and opened it. A group of specialists walked into the Oval Office.

"I'm sure you recognize the fine people from previous sessions. We have kept the team together, one, for consistency and, two, because, frankly, they are the best," the president said.

The team handed out the assessment report, labeled, 'The New America—Top Secret'.

"Alright, let's get started," the president said.

Somewhere Down that Crazy River

Sarah and Sasha slept as the canoe slowly followed the current down the winding river. The girls lay on blankets and groundsheets inside the canoe.

The pace was slow but Bobby had expected that. He had done the math and figured a good six to seven hours to be out to Vermilion Bay based on the distance and the speed of the current.

What he hadn't anticipated was how much the silence and the waiting would affect him. The minutes gnawed away at him. Every sound caused him to bristle. He knew the danger that he and his two daughters were under until they reached open water and the safety of Jerome's boat.

A few hours into the ride, Bobby felt something bump up against the canoe. He didn't react at first, assuming it was just something floating in the water but, after several more bumps, he needed to see what was going on.

He carefully lifted some of the branches from above him. He looked down. There was something there, in the water, bouncing up against the boat. In the darkness, it was difficult to make out exactly what it was.

He waited for a couple more bumps and then took out his cell phone. He peered out one more time. The coast appeared clear. He turned the cell phone light on and shone it down on what was bumping up against the boat. Whatever it was, it was big and dark.

Bobby reached down and pushed on it with one hand while holding the light in the other hand. The object bobbed down under the water and resurfaced. As it popped back up, he could see what it was. It was an older woman. She was dead and was burned and badly disfigured.

Bobby recoiled. He quickly dropped back down into the canoe, hiding away from the face on the water. Another bump hit the boat and then another. He realized that the impact and the sound risked waking Sasha.

He looked over the edge of the canoe again, peering back into whatever horror may have been there. He shone his phone light across the water's surface, illuminating the extent of the scene. It wasn't one body, it was a dozen, maybe more, all burned, all floating down the river, just as Bobby as his daughters were. The difference was, those in the water were now free of the fear of what may come next. Bobby's fate, and that of his daughters, was as unclear as the current that slowly pulled them downstream.

Bobby reached out from the canoe one more time and pushed the body away. It slowly drifted away. He lay back down, adjusted the branches, and closed his eye. He put his hands over his ears and began to quietly hum an old childhood song

Eventually, Bobby fell asleep. He found himself in a dream. In the dream, the canoe washed up onto Marsh Island Refuge. The boat impacted the shoreline and jostled Bobby, Sarah, and Sasha. The three of them popped through the branches and looked around. It was dark out.

"Where are we, Daddy?" Sasha asked.

"I think we are on Marsh Island," Bobby replied, looking around.

Sarah said nothing. She simply sat and looked towards the center of the island.

"Let's get out of the boat and onto land," Bobby said, and stepped out of the canoe. He waded into the two-foot-deep water and pulled the canoe fully ashore.

He helped the two girls out of the canoe and then secured it.

"Daddy, what are we doing here?" Sasha asked.

"We're waiting for Uncle Jerome to pick us up, remember?"

"Oh, yeah."

Sarah continued to stare straight ahead.

"Sarah?" Bobby asked.

She didn't reply. She began to walk toward the island's heart. Bobby and Sasha quickly followed her.

"Sarah, where are you going?" Bobby asked.

Sarah stopped, turned, and said nothing. She pointed toward the heart of the island and started to walk again. Her skin seemed an odd gray.

Bobby and Sasha continued to follow Sarah. While it was night, there were no stars in the sky. There was a tinge of smoke in the air.

The three walked for some ten minutes through a mix of grassy areas and short vegetation until they walked into a small wooded area.

"Daddy, what is Sarah doing?" Sasha asked.

"I don't know but she seems to know so I guess we'll follow her."

They walked through the woods for a few minutes before they came out into an opening where a spectacular Louisiana home sat on the edge of a bayou. The sky in the opening was completely clear. The stars shone in such a way that it caught Bobby and Sasha's attention.

The sight was so mesmerizing that the two of them nearly tripped. They caught themselves and hustled after Sarah who was relentlessly moving forward.

As they drew closer to the home, Bobby could see a man, dressed all in dark gray, sitting on a rocking chair on the front porch. He slowly rocked back and forth while watching Bobby and the two girls approach.

"Ah, Sarah. Welcome, we have been expecting you," the gray man said.

Sarah quickly ran up the stairs to the porch and went to sit in the gray man's lap.

Bobby was stunned. Sasha looked up at Bobby and asked, "Who is that man?"

"I'm not sure, Sasha, but we are going to find out."

He and Sasha walked over to the gray man. As they did, Bobby tried to get a good look at the man's face. Between the lighting and the odd movements of the man, he was unable to get a clear view of him.

"Sarah, come here," Bobby ordered.

Sarah turned and looked at the gray man. He nodded. Sarah stood up and took a step toward Bobby and Sasha.

"Who the hell are you?" Bobby asked.

The gray man laughed. "Who and what I am is not important right now. What's important is that you are here. Please, come around back, the festivities are about to begin."

He got up and walked around the porch to the back of the house. Sarah followed close behind, as did Bobby and Sasha.

When they reached the back, they found a large deck that led down to a backyard covered in grass. In the middle of the yard was a fire pyre. Many people were sitting around the pyre on benches and chairs.

Bobby looked around all of them with the odd skin color that Sarah now had. Sarah ran down and grabbed a chair near the pyre. The gray man walked over to Bobby. He took a cigar case out of his pocket.

"Bobby, I'm glad you are here. Can I offer you a cigar? They are Cuban, of course," the gray man asked.

Bobby gave him a shocked look. "No, I'll pass. What the hell is going on here?"

The gray man put his cigar in his mouth and casually lit it from an old-school lighter. Bobby caught a glimpse of the lighter as the gray man placed it back into his pocket. There were tiny human faces on it, faces that were moving. He was certain that he could see that some of the faces were screaming.

"Bobby, what is going on here is exactly what was expected. You've lost your wife and your father, not to mention many friends and family. What did you do while they were suffering?"

Bobby looked away, doing his best to ignore the question.

The gray man blew a larger smoke cloud out. For a moment, the smoke cloud took on a demonic form of a head with horns before it slipped away in the warm evening breeze.

"That's right, stand by your beliefs, Bobby."

"So, what? There was a lot of confusion about the virus and the vaccines. It wasn't a black-and-white decision. I made a choice that I thought was best for us."

The gray man turned and caught eyes with Bobby. "And how did that turn out, Bobby?"

"Fuck you. You know nothing about me," Bobby yelled.

The gray man laughed a little. "*Au contraire*, I know everything about you," he said darkly.

He then walked away and made his way down to the fire pyre. Bobby and Sasha walked to the railing of the deck.

"Welcome all. This is your night. Time has come, let us rejoice!" the gray man yelled.

As he spoke, the fire pyre erupted into a huge flame. There was a loud cheer from those around the fire.

Bobby looked down to see Sarah moving toward the fire. He then noticed that everyone on the grass level was also moving.

Music began to play. It was the Doors' *Light my Fire*.

"Shit," Bobby said and quickly headed for the stairs down to the grass.

He was too late. Sarah, like the rest of them down on the grass, stepped into the growing fire.

"NO!" Bobby screamed and ran to the fire's edge. He tried to reach in but found himself restrained. He looked back to see the gray man holding his arm.

"You care now, do you? Where were you when you could have changed this path? Sarah will not live—this is how this universe works. It provides free choice, but with choice comes repercussions," the gray man said while holding Bobby's arm tightly.

Bobby turned to yell at the gray man but found himself sitting, alone, in the canoe in the middle of the Gulf of Mexico, bobbing amongst the waves.

A loud noise woke him from the dream. Another sound shattered the quiet night. This one, Bobby knew well—it was a gunshot.

"Shit," he muttered.

He lay as still as he could, hoping whoever was shooting was doing so randomly and not targeting them.

Quiet…

Another gunshot. This one clipped the back of the canoe. Sasha woke up. Bobby reached over and put his hand across her mouth and whispered, "Shhh."

He could feel the terror rising in Sasha just as it was rising in him.

Another shot rang out. Bobby heard the bullet whistle just above the canoe. He tightened his grip on Sasha's mouth until she squirmed in pain.

"Geez, Dougie, why the fuck you shooting at a log? You just wasting ammo," a voice in the distance said.

"Shit, Dale, I'm just practicing."

"Well, I say you save your practice for when people try and get through the county lines. We ain't got an unlimited supply of bullets, you know."

"Alright, just one more."

"Yeah, but that's it."

Bobby closed his eyes and prayed.

A shot rang out.

"Shit, yeah, bull's-eye."

The bullet ripped into the middle of the canoe and right through Sarah. She never even woke up.

Safe House

After a much longer and more dangerous walk than Jimmy had anticipated, they arrived at the safe house.

"Gentlemen, and I use that term loosely, this is our safe house for the day. There are six bedrooms here, all with two beds, so there is plenty of room for all. I ain't your maid. You guys figure your shit out but be ready to leave here at midnight. You leave this place during the day, you ain't coming back in. You all know the price you pay in getting caught," DeSantos yelled at them.

"We good, brother," Big Al said.

"Alright, I got the room at the end of this hall. I catch any of you shits trying to get in, I blow you into the next world," DeSantos said, waving his handgun around.

No one said anything. DeSantos walked down the hallway as if he owned the place.

"Come on, Jimmy, I've been here before. We'll bunk together," Big Al said and led Jimmy down the hall to a side bedroom.

"I'll grab this bed, you can have that one. Put your shit on it and no one will touch it. There is a code here," Big Al said.

Jimmy slung his backpack off and tossed it down onto the bed. The backpack bounced and the springs squeaked out from the impact. Jimmy looked down at the bed and knew it wasn't going to be a good sleep.

"Come on, let's go grab a few drinks with the boys first. We can grab some sleep later," Big Al said smiling.

Drinks, sure, why not? thought Jimmy. "Sure, let's do it."

The two of them joined most of the guys back in the main room. A couple of guys had decided that they were better off grabbing some early sleep.

DeSantos slid a case of beer onto the old wooden coffee table. "Drink up, boys," he said and then ripped a beer out of the case for himself.

Jimmy and Big Al grabbed beers as well and sat down.

"So, what's up tonight, DeSantos?" Big Al asked.

He downed half his beer before replying. "We got a service van gonna pick us up nearby. It's a company that services the rail lines. They gonna get us to a station where we got friendlies. It's still a yellow zone there so it will be easy to get there cause there won't be any checks."

He downed the rest of his beer.

"From there, we gonna get on a cargo train heading north. The train will get us right up near Rochester and into a green zone. My people will make sure that we are well hidden but you all gotta be extra careful cause at the green check they are gonna board the train and check everything."

Jimmy looked around the faces in the room. Half the guys were like Jimmy; they had lived through enough shit in their lives that this didn't faze them. The other half were tagalongs, guys that Jimmy would stay well away from if the shit hit the fan.

From there, the conversation evolved as would be expected. The virus, America, and finally how to find a good woman in a time of a pandemic.

Four beers in, Jimmy decided it was his bedtime. He bid the group goodbye for now and wandered back down the hallway to his room.

He closed the door and got himself down onto the bed. It was just as expected—sinking in the middle with the odd spring poking up. Nevertheless, he was asleep in minutes, given the night they had just gone through. He needed sleep; he knew the next night was going to be even harder.

Coming Clean

The shift ended quietly for Will and Carlos. As it did, Will's anxiety crept up. He knew what was awaiting him at the end of the shift.

"Will, you ready to do this? I think you should, just like we talked about. It was defense; I'm sure folks will get that," Carlos said.

Will fretted a little. Was he ready? Was anybody ready to fess up to shooting someone? He looked over at Carlos. He loved the guy. He never really had many close friends in life; he had always been a bit of a loner. A piece of him didn't want to disappoint him.

"Yeah, I guess I am."

Carlos put his big arm around Will. "It will work out, you'll see."

The two of them walked over to the shift lead.

"Sir, I have something to tell you," Will said sheepishly.

"Well, what is it?" the lead replied.

"I shot someone."

"WHAT? When? Tonight?"

"No, two days ago, at Costco."

"Jesus, Will, why the hell didn't you tell us last night? You should not have been on duty. Wait here, I need to make a couple of calls."

"Don't worry, Will, it will be okay. I'll grab a ride back to town with Mark. Call me when you know what is going on," Carlos said and hugged Will.

Will watched Carlos walk over to the rest of the guys. He wished Carlos could stay with him for the process. Moreso, he wished he had never tried to play the big man and pull that gun out.

A couple of minutes later, the lead returned.

"Will, I'm gonna have to take your gun and ask you to stay here until the sheriff arrives."

Will slowly handed his gun over. "Okay, I understand."

"How about you wait over in the guardhouse for now?" the lead suggested.

"Yeah, okay."

Will wandered over to the guardhouse feeling pretty crappy about his life.

"Not headed home yet, Will?" one of the guys in the guardhouse asked.

"Hmmm, no, I'm meeting someone here before I head back."

"Ah, hope it's a young lady." The man smiled.

Will feigned a grin back and found a seat in the corner.

As he sat and waited he reflected how the world had changed so quickly over the last few weeks. *I'm just changing too* he thought. The problem was, even he didn't really believe that.

After a good 30 minute, stressful wait, the sheriff arrived. Will watched the car roll up. His heart skipped a couple of beats, at least.

"Will James?" the sheriff asked.

Will stood up and said, "That's me."

"Alright, come with me."

Will walked out with a few sets of eyes on him. It was pretty clear that he hadn't been waiting for a girl. That just further drove his anxiety.

They walked out to the sheriff's car. "Will, how about we get into the car?"

Will walked around to the passenger side and got in.

"Will, I need to hear what happened, from you. I already got the story from the site," the sheriff asked,

Will jostled for a moment, trying to capture his courage.

"Well, I went down to the Costco to pick up a few things on account that so many places were closed. When I got there, there was some kind of a battle going on at the door cause of masks. The security guard was pushing people around and, well, then he assaulted me," Will said with a little more emotion than he had expected.

The sheriff gave Will an uncomfortably long look. "Okay, to be honest, that is pretty consistent with reports we have from the incident. So, you shot him in self-defense is what you're telling me?"

Will paused for a moment.

"Yes," Will replied. "I was worried about what he would do to others," he quickly added.

The sheriff took out a pad of paper and a pen. He made a few notes. The lead wandered over as the sheriff was making notes.

"So, what's the verdict, Bill? Hate to lose one of our men," he asked the sheriff.

The sheriff finished up his notes and put his pad away.

"I guess we'll see what a judge has to say but seems like we might just have a case of self-defense here."

Will quiet breathed a sigh of relief.

"That's what I was thinking too. How soon before he can get in front of a judge? We're gonna need every man we got soon enough, I figure."

The sheriff smiled at the lead. "Yeah, I know, I'm with you guys. I just gotta make sure these things get done right. I figure we can get him in front of old Judge Dave tomorrow. We ain't doing the regular courthouse thing no more cause of the virus, so I'll just get Will over to Dave's place sometime tomorrow afternoon," the sheriff replied.

"Thanks, Bill. You and I both know we got a war coming."

"That we do."

The sheriff turned back to Will. "Look, I'm gonna need to keep your gun and any others you have at home until this thing is sorted. I'll follow you to your house and you can give 'em to me there."

Will nodded. All in all, the situation was turning out a lot better than he had expected. The world was changing and it seemed to Will that the more it did, the more he liked it.

Will did as he was told. He followed Sheriff Bill back into town and to Will's, house. The sheriff walked into the house with Will and grabbed his two other guns.

"Look, Will, I'm not going to detain you. The truth is we mostly shut the jail down, except for a few real bad folks. So, I'm going to ask you to stay here, in your place, Will. Can you do that for me?" the sheriff asked quite directly.

"Yes, sir, I most certainly can."

The sheriff patted Will on the shoulder. "Good man," he said and took the two guns out to his car.

Will watched as the sheriff packed the guns into the trunk of the squad car and drove off. He then picked up his phone and called his new bestie, Carlos.

"So, what happened?" Carlos asked.

"The sheriff took my guns but says it looks like it's might be self-defense, just like we talked about. I'm gonna see a judge tomorrow afternoon to get it all sorted."

"See, I told you, buddy. Where are you now?"

"Sheriff told me to stay home."

"Well, heck buddy, I'm grabbing some beers and heading over to see you," Carlos exclaimed.

Will smiled ear to ear. "Yes, please."

He hung up and walked over to the window. He smiled again as he looked out over the world, his world, one he was liking more and more every day.

Tragedy Down Stream

Bobby continued to hold his hand over Sasha's mouth as tears rolled down his face. He knew if he or Sasha cried out, the next gunshots would cut right through them.

"Sasha, please, just hold on a little longer and we'll be away from trouble. Can you do that for me, sweetie?"

Sasha squirmed a little and then nodded. Bobby took his hand off her mouth and then kissed her on the forehead.

They floated for some five minutes in dead silence. Water was seeping into the canoe through the hole made by the same bullet that killed Sarah.

Finally, when Bobby felt it was safe, he lifted some of the branches and took a peek out. They were where he had originally planned to be. They were floating toward the end of a four-mile cutoff.

There was some three to four inches of water in the canoe. Water, which had mixed with Sarah's blood.

Sasha was quietly crying, holding Sarah's head in her lap as the canoe bobbed along with the increasing current.

"Sasha, I'm gonna guide the canoe to the shore now. We are past the county guard line. We need to get ashore and call Uncle Jerome," he whispered to Sasha.

She looked up at him, eyes streaming tears. "It doesn't matter anymore. Sarah's dead, Daddy."

True, he thought. The fact was, though, there were still the two of them to save.

"Sasha, I still need to save you. I need to save you for Mommy and Sarah," he replied while holding her face in his hands.

She wiped her eyes and then nodded, "Yes, we do, Daddy."

Bobby pulled the one short oar he had tucked into the canoe out. He reached over the side and, without sitting up fully, stuck it in the water.

From there he sculled the oar slowly working the canoe to the western side of the four-mile cutoff.

They skimmed the shore until they reached the gap out to Vermilion Bay was visible. He forced the canoe up against the shore. He carefully got out and pulled it onto land.

"Come on, Sasha, it's time to get out."

"What about Sarah?" she asked.

"I'll get her out."

"Okay, Daddy."

Bobby reached down, took Sasha by the hand, and helped her out of the canoe. He hugged her, deep and long, once she was on the shore.

"Can you hold on to the canoe for me?" he asked.

Sasha got down onto her knees and grabbed hold of the canoe with both hands. Bobby put one foot into the canoe and gently lifted Sarah's soaked body from the bottom. Rigor mortis had not fully set in yet but her body was no longer that of the happy, warm child Bobby remembered.

Bobby placed Sarah's body on the ground. As he did, he began to cry uncontrollably and slumped to the ground with her. Sasha put her arms around her father and shared in his cry.

Eventually, Bobby got up and hugged Sasha. He then took his phone out and made a call.

"Jerome, it's Bobby. We are at the pick-up but we have a serious problem."

A New America

The last of the experts wrapped up their assessment. The president thanked them and Jim led them out of the room.

"Thoughts? This is a momentous moment in our history. I understand the impact; we do not come to this point lightly. We have a major decision to make, one that will fundamentally change this country. The truth is, this virus, our broken political system, and personal agendas have already created the break. We need to recognize that and, more importantly, take the difficult decisions and actions to save a core of what we were in hopes of eventually saving it all. Jim put the projector on please," the president said.

The lights went off and a projector flashed the map of America up on the wall. It was a map that every American knew from childhood.

"Folks, based on the detailed assessment we all just sat through, this is what is recommended for America going forward. Jim," the president said, looking over at Jim.

The image changed. A new map appeared. This one was colored in green and red, not by state but by county and region.

"What we have here is the 'Green America'. It's an America where we have confidence we can maintain control and, more importantly, ensure stability and safety to the citizens. The floor is open," the president said.

"As I look at this map, I'm reminded of the fall of Rome. I remember, as a child, looking at the map of the Roman Empire at its peak and being amazed not only as to the size of the empire but by the incredible diversity and the stability, the empire brought to the world that was savage in so many ways. America once was this as well. We created a nation that was the envy of the world. We were a beacon of hope at a time when the world needed it and, just as the Roman Empire slipped away, now, so is ours it seems," the House Minority Leader said.

The room was silent for a moment. A sense of reality was setting in.

"As hard as this is, we all know it is the right thing to do. The question is, how do we make this happen? We are on new ground here. I presume this will require further deployment of the military. Under what jurisdiction would it be managed? Is this the National Guard, Homeland Security, or the United States Armed Forces?" one of the team asked.

"The short answer is, yes. We have the chairman of the armed forces and the head of Homeland Security on board. We are discussing the role of the National Guard at various state levels. What we envision is a unified homeland force, coordinated by Homeland Security and the Pentagon. Its mandate will be to manage these new borders," the president said.

"Would we not require Congressional approval?" someone else asked.

"Technically we should; however, given that Congress is not sitting presently and the fact that we have numerous openings in Congress due to virus deaths, it would be effectively impossible. Jim, what's the latest count on vacancies?"

"We have lost twelve members of Congress and six Senators over the last three weeks. The majority, in both cases, are Republicans. Ten of the twelve in Congress are Republican and five of the six Senators are as well. This is not a surprise given their view of sensible protections versus personal rights."

"So, what we have is essentially a non-functioning government infrastructure at the time of the greatest challenge to our nation," the president said.

"Okay, we declare a national state of emergency, deploy the new national force across borders of the red zones on this map, I'm guessing," the House Minority Leader said.

"That is the current plan. We will use the state of emergency to push the executive order through. Now, it isn't going to go over well, as you have probably surmised. We believe the best strategy is to make the declaration and roll the troops out very quickly," the president replied.

"What will the troops' mandate be?" the House Minority Leader asked.

"It will be a defensive role. They will take defensive positions at every transit point across the map. They will deploy overnight and quickly establish physical posts. In many cases, we already have the National Guard established. Some have been there since we set up the red, yellow, and green zones."

"What do you mean by 'transit points'?" one of the team asked.

"Anywhere that it is reasonably possible to cross the new border. We have highways and main roads covered already. We have some of the rural and subsidiary roads covered as well. We have some of the rail lines and some of the waterways. Those are areas that will need to be tightened up. Additionally, we will need to find ways to plug up the little-used pathways. These will be more difficult and we expect there will be an uptick in border crossing in those areas until we get a handle on them."

"How much of a military increase do you anticipate?" the House Minority Leader asked.

"We will need to triple the boots we currently have on the ground at a minimum."

"Boots on the ground. Our boots, on our soil," one of the team replied.

After an uncomfortable quiet, the president replied, "Yes, our boots on our soil."

"Jesus," the House Minority Leader muttered.

"This, based on the assessment we all just heard, is the lesser of two evils," the president said.

"We do seem to be living in evil times," someone replied.

"I guess we don't have a lot of choices here. When do we do this?" the House Minority Leader asked.

"I'm waiting for a final preparedness date from the Joint Chiefs but it will be very soon," the president said.

"I guess we have a short time to appreciate the America we've known our whole lives," the House Minority Leader said.

"Helen, with all due respect, I believe we lost that America some time ago," Jim said.

The House Minority Leader looked at Jim harshly and then relented. "You're probably right, Jim. Frankly, it's difficult to be one of the architects of dismantling America."

"We all feel that way, Helen," the president said.

Everyone nodded; there was a visible emotion in the room.

"We have broken with the traditional process out of need; however, I want this room, this group, to be in sync with what we plan to do. I want a vote, here and now," the president said.

"I agree, let's make this officially unofficial," the House Minority Leader said.

"A show of hands. All in favor of implementing the New America Plan, raise your hand and say aye," Jim said.

It was unanimous. Everyone raised their hand although the confidence in some was wavering.

"It's confirmed. The vote is unanimous," Jim confirmed.

"May God protect us," one of the team members said.

They all got up, shook hands, and began to make their way out of the room.

The House Minority Leader sought out the president. "I hope history will show that we did what was right," he said as he shook the president's hand.

"Helen, I truly do too."

A Changing Relationship

Will woke with a pretty decent hangover. He got himself out of bed and made his way into the living room. Carlos lay there, on the couch, likely as hungover as Will was.

He was just about to smack him on the shoulder to wake him up when he paused. He stepped back and sat down on the chair near the front window and looked over at Carlos. The sun had already risen and its rays cast through the cheap sheers that hung in the room. The light lay upon Carlos in what was a slightly provocative manner.

Will leaned forward and looked closely at the man. He was likely in his early thirties and had a little Hispanic in him. He was tall, maybe six foot two, and solidly built.

It was funny, Will thought. He had always had an odd attraction to men like Carlos. He was pretty sure he wasn't gay but, in truth, he had never really been that attracted to women. He was a small man and he found comfort in the company of men like Carlos.

He got up awkwardly and walked over to the couch. He stood for a moment, unsure as to what he was doing. He reached down to touch his face. Carlos' eyes snapped open.

"Hey, shit, buddy, what a good time last night," Carlos exclaimed.

Will recoiled slightly. "Yeah, yeah it sure was. You want some breakfast?"

Carlos quickly sat up. "Hell yeah."

"Alright, let's go do it," Will said with a forced smile.

The two wandered into the kitchen and Will pulled out everything that was needed to get a good breakfast going.

"Carlos, sit down. Let me get this ready. You brought the beer last night," Will said.

"You sure, buddy?"

"Yeah, for sure." Will smiled.

Carlos grabbed one of the rickety wooden chairs around the small oval table in the kitchen. The chair cracked a little as he sat down. The two of them laughed.

Will finished preparing the breakfast. It wasn't anything gourmet, just a few eggs, a little bacon, and some grits. Supplies were light at Will's just as they were all over town.

"So, you think you'll be good this afternoon?" Carlos said.

"I think so. The sheriff seemed to want me to be."

"That's good. I'd be pretty busted up if you got kicked out."

Carlos reached over and grabbed a piece of bacon off Will's plate with a smile.

"You don't mind, do ya?"

Will smiled back. "Of course not."

"Hey, you know, the lead said there is a war coming to the sheriff," Will said.

"Maybe there is, Will," Carlos replied, chewing away on bacon.

Will looked out the window. "I don't know. Yeah, maybe there is," he absent-mindedly repeated.

The phone rang. "Will here."

"Will, it's Sheriff Bill. We got you your court date this afternoon, 3 pm. I'll come by around 2:30 pm to get you," the sheriff said.

"Wow, thanks. Yes, I'll be ready for sure."

Will hung up and looked at Carlos. "I got the judge meeting this afternoon."

"Shit, that's good," Carlos stood up and hugged Will hard.

Will smiled ear to ear.

Riding the Rails

Jimmy found himself shaken awake by someone. It was Big Al.

"Jimmy, brother, it's time to get ready."

"Shit, man, what time is it?"

"It's about 11:30. We gonna have to walk about forty minutes, DeSantos told us. That's where we gonna get picked up."

"Yeah, sure, okay. I guess I'm up," Jimmy said, forcing himself to get up.

He was sorer than he had realized. He was in pretty good shape but the group had walked a long way the day before, certainly more than he had in some time.

"Damn, I am sore today," he said as he straightened himself out.

Big Al laughed. "You ain't the only one."

The two men packed their backpacks up tight again and threw them over their shoulders.

"Alright, let's go join the rest of them," Jimmy said.

The two of them made their way down the hall to the living room area. It was a bit of a mess. A couple of cases of beer were finished and empty bottles were strewn about the room. Marijuana smoke hung about in the air.

"Ah, the two sleepyheads," DeSantos said, smiling.

Big Al shoved himself into the couch between two of the guys to a few groans.

"Jimmy, you need a bump before we go?" DeSantos asked.

Jimmy could see there was a mirror on the coffee table with a few lines set up on it. Normally he would jump all over it but, given what was ahead of them, he knew he needed his wits about him.

"Nah, man, it's only gonna make me want more," Jimmy grinned.

"I hear ya," DeSantos replied and bent over to do a line.

Jimmy looked around at the crew. Several of them were still drunk. He knew that not everyone was going to get through the coming night. He also knew he was going to keep himself well away from that group.

DeSantos took one last line and then stood up quickly. "Alright, it's time to rock and roll, boys."

Everyone got up. Some with more pep in their step than others.

"We gotta be careful who we stick around tonight," Big Al whispered to Jimmy.

"Yeah, I know."

Everyone lined up by the front door, hoodies, and backpacks on.

DeSantos peered out the eye hole. "Alright, let's go. We got about a forty-minute walk or so to the pick-up. Same routine as yesterday. I'll lead and I want you all to spread out and stay fucking quiet."

He opened the door and the group quietly slipped out into the dark.

Jimmy and Big Al got themselves right up behind DeSantos and Leon. They both knew that it was likely the safest place possible.

DeSantos led the group through some old laneways and then onto a train track.

They walked quietly in the dark. The area seemed safer than it was back in the Barrio but if any of them were to be grabbed by the local authorities, they would be thrown right into jail. None of them had an ID coding that allowed them in a yellow zone, let alone a green one. DeSantos was right. Heads down and quiet was the way to go.

About thirty-five minutes in, loud voices could be heard from behind them. It didn't take long to figure out that some of the guys down at the end of the line were being taken down.

"We gotta run," Big Al yelled back to Jimmy and took off.

Jimmy began to run as well. In a few minutes, he reached the service hut by the train tracks. A cube van with no plates was waiting there. DeSantos and Leon were there as well. Jimmy and Big Al quickly joined them.

"Shit, some of them dumb fucks got tripped up," DeSantos said as he nervously looked down the tracks.

He looked down at his watch and back up at the rail track. "You two get in the van. We'll grab the next few and we're gonna have to get out of here."

Jimmy and Big Al climbed into the back of the van. A young woman was sitting quietly there already. She just stared at the floor.

All three of them sat quietly, patiently, and nervously waiting for the van to leave. About three minutes later, DeSantos jumped in the van with Mickey, Phil, and two more of the crew.

He closed and locked the back doors and banged hard on the side of the van.

The van started up and sped off.

"Two of them dumb asses got grabbed," DeSantos said, quite pissed off.

"This is why we don't tell you lot much in advance. All them fucking government dicks might find out is that we will be on a cargo train. They won't know anything about where and what train. We'll be long gone before them shits figure anything out," he laughed.

Jimmy looked around at those who were left. Not surprisingly, it was mainly those that Jimmy had figured were more like him.

The crew sat quietly in the back of the van as it sped along, going who knew where.

Eventually, the van stopped. DeSantos got up and opened the back door. "Okay, we're here. You all gonna follow Leon out to the train yard."

Everyone did as they were told, no questions asked. No one was interested in questioning; all they wanted to do was to keep moving.

DeSantos pulled the gun out of his belt and stood watch. Once the group was out of the van and in the train yard, he quickly came and joined them.

"Alright, this station is rarely used anymore, just a couple of times a week for cargo. Tonight is one of those nights a train runs out of here. We're gonna pack you all up as cargo. It's gonna be a little uncomfortable but it's the only way to make sure we are all safe. If you got claustrophobia, you might just want to call that out now," Leon said.

The crew looked at each other. No one spoke again. No one was ready to give up their ticket to freedom.

DeSantos and Leon led the group to a rail car and everyone was helped up into it.

Inside there were two new people. They had boxes and packing materials.

"Get ready to be packed. Who's up first?" Leon asked.

Big Al put his hand up and stepped forward. He then looked back at Jimmy and smiled. "See you on the other side, brother."

Jimmy smiled back. He hoped he would see him again and on the other side.

Big Al was put in a big box. He had a large chair under him with packing material under and around him. He was given water and a snack for the ride. A wooden frame was put in next and some stacked chairs were placed on top of the frame. A liquid was sprayed on Big Al and inside the box. The box was closed up and professionally sealed by the two new people.

Jimmy was up next. He was placed in a mattress box. He had a mattress underneath him, a wooden frame above him, and a few more mattresses on the frame. He was also given water and a snack and sprayed before his box was closed up. He wasn't a claustrophobic person by nature but he was quickly impacted by the darkness. He would have taken his phone out and used the light but he had been forced to hand it over at the safe house.

He laid back and closed his eyes.

About fifteen minutes later, he felt the train start to roll slowly forward. He closed his eyes again. He knew the next eight hours were going to be mentally grueling.

A Rescue a Little too Late

"This sounds serious, Bobby," Jerome said.

"It is, Jerome. Sarah is dead. She was shot while we were leaving the county."

"Shit, man, are you sure she's dead?"

"Yeah, I'm damn sure."

"Hey, Bobby, I'm real sorry. If you're at the pick-up point we are nearby. We've had to move around a little. There are a bunch of patrol boats around but we got the fastest boat out here."

Bobby settled himself down. It would be easy to just fall apart, let everything go, and mourn Sarah but he had Sasha as well and he needed to get her to safety.

"Yes, we are here and we still need your help."

"Okay, we are on our way. It's pretty hairy down there so we will be coming in dark and quiet. Keep your eyes open. See you in about ten minutes."

Bobby hung up and turned back to see Sarah's body again. Sasha was holding her.

He sat down beside the two of them. "Sasha, I'm so sorry. I caused this. I was stupid and weak," he said very emotionally.

"Well, you're still here, Daddy," she smiled.

He was still there. That fact made the whole situation even worse. His pigheadedness had not cost him his life; it took his wife and daughter instead. Neither of them had a say in the decisions that ultimately cost their lives.

"Is Uncle Jerome coming?"

"Yes, he is."

"That's good."

Bobby left Sasha with Sarah and moved down to the shoreline to look for the boat. As he watched, he could see what Jerome meant. He noticed several boats appearing to be patrolling out in Vermilion Bay.

Out of the dark, Bobby made out Jerome's boat as it quietly glided toward them. Bobby waved his hands.

The boat slowly turned its side toward them and dropped anchor. Bobby's phone rang.

"Hey, Bobby, we need you to come out to the boat. The water is too shallow for us to get in any closer. Can you run out to us in the canoe?"

Bobby paused for a moment. "No, the canoe is unusable."

"Hmmm, alright, we'll send over the raft. We gotta move quickly. Lots of boats out."

"Yeah, I saw some of them. We'll be ready for you," Bobby said and hung up.

"Sasha, we need to lift Sarah and help get her onto the raft that Uncle Jerome is sending."

"Okay, Daddy."

The two of them picked up Sarah; her body had become stiff, her skin further gray, and her face gaunt. Bobby looked away. The last thing he wanted was that image in his head after he had effectively killed her. If Sasha had noticed, she elected to ignore it. The two girls were close, really close. He worried that Sasha wasn't processing what was happening. In some ways, he envied her at that moment.

The raft quietly and skillfully drifted through the dark, murky water. The lone driver pushed the front edge onto the shore.

Bobby, with Sasha's help, lifted Sarah's small stiff frame in the raft."Oh, boy," the driver leaked out as he took hold of Sarah.

Bobby looked at him with disdain."Hey, sorry man. Caught me off guard is all," the driver said.

"It caught us all off guard," Bobby replied harshly.

The driver, with Bobby, settled Sarah's body on the bottom of the raft. Bobby helped Sasha into the raft.

The driver started the small electric motor and turned the raft toward Jerome's boat."It won't be long," the driver said nervously.

Bobby nodded.

The raft glided slowly away from the shore. Bobby had rarely left Louisiana in his life. It had always, happily, been his home but the world was different now as was Louisiana.

They reach the boat and pulled up to the backside. Jerome and another man reached down and secured the raft. The driver got out and helped Sasha and then Bobby out of the raft.

Jerome looked down into the raft at Sarah. He hugged Bobby. "I am so sorry."

Bobby hugged him back very emotionally. "Can we get her out of the raft?"

"Of course. How about you and I do that," Jerome said.

"I'd appreciate that."

With the driver and the other man holding the raft, Bobby stepped back in and lifted Sarah by the shoulder while Jerome lifted her legs. Her body had further stiffened. It was no longer his little girl.

"Let's take her below deck," Jerome said.

"Yes, please."

"Guys, get the raft back up on the back. We gotta get out of here," Jerome yelled.

Jerome and Bobby carefully carried Sarah down into the galley area and placed her on a couch. Sasha followed them down.

"Daddy, can I stay with her?" she asked.

"Yes, that would be nice."

Jerome grabbed some blankets and placed them over Sarah, however, he left her face visible, for Sasha.

"I need to get to the wheel; we gotta get going," Jerome said.

Bobby looked over at Sasha and Sarah. "I'll come with you."

The two of them headed up to the bridge. Jerome started the engines up and slowly pushed out into Vermilion Bay.

"We gotta go slow and quiet here. Most of the patrols are in and around the bay here. It isn't just government anymore. There are militia groups out there too now, trying to keep the government out," Jerome said.

"How long will it take to get to Port Arthur?"

"We have to take a long route, around Marsh Island and out East Cote Blanche Bay. The passage on the west side is too narrow. It's a choke point. Given that, we got a good six hours to go."

"I'd like to stay up here for a while if that's okay," Bobby said.

"Of course, cousin."

Bobby sat down on the little couch behind Jerome and looked out over the horizon. It wasn't long before he noticed a landmass.

"What is that?" he asked Jerome.

"Marsh Island."

Given the dream Bobby had just had about the island, he took a closer look. It seemed there was light emanating from somewhere inside the island. He figured it was just a remnant memory from the dream.

"Jerome, is it me or is there a light coming up out of the island?"

Jerome turned and looked at the island. He paused for a moment.

"There does seem to be a light coming out of there. That's weird, the island is a wildlife refuge."

"It's not so weird to me," Bobby said quietly to himself.

A Not So Surprising Judgment

The sheriff showed up as planned. Will was watching from the window and as soon as he saw the car, he hustled out the door.

The sheriff got out of the car and came around to open the back door. Will noticed a deputy sitting in the front passenger seat.

"Don't worry, Will, this is standard," the sheriff said, noticing the concern on Will's face.

Will got in the back of the car and they drove off.

"Will, we're going to see the judge today. I want you to tell him exactly what you told me and be honest when he asks you questions," the sheriff said as he drove.

"Okay, I will."

They drove for a couple more minutes until they hit a red light.

The sheriff turned and looked at Will.

"Will, we are all patriots here. The man that assaulted you, he's no patriot. I don't know how he got a security job with his criminal background. You say the right things today and you can continue to be a patriot. You understand me, right?" the sheriff said with an intensity Will had not seen before.

"I understand."

The light turned green and the conversation ended.

They arrived at the judge's house just before 3 pm. The deputy got out and walked up to the house.

"Deputy Williams is going to check that the judge is ready. We have a lot of new, improvised, procedures."

Will nodded politely. He had no doubt there were a lot of changes to many of the procedures of late.

A couple of minutes later, the deputy stepped out of the house and waved them in.

"Alright, you're up, Will," the sheriff said and got out of the squad car.

The sheriff opened the door and led Will up to the house. Once they reached the door, they were met by two large court bailiffs.

"We need to see your ID," one of the men said.

Will showed the man his driver's license, the only real ID he owned. The man looked it over and handed it back to Will.

"That's fine. I need to frisk you now," the bailiff said.

Will put his arms up in the air and let the man frisk him. Will looked around the house; it was spectacular. They stood in a foyer that was larger than Will's little house.

"He's clean," the bailiff said.

Another bailiff walked into the foyer and asked Will and the sheriff to follow him. They walked into a large office just off the foyer.

Will had never seen the kind of wood the judge had in his office. It looked exotic and expensive. For him, wood was just wood; it made the frame and foundation for homes and other things, he had never thought of it as decoration.

Around the room were many pictures of presidents and state governors. All of them were Republican.

"Will James?" the bailiff asked.

The question caught Will off guard for a moment. He had let himself get caught up in someone else's success, again.

"Yes, yes I am," Will stuttered.

"Relax, Will. Have a seat here. We are here to hear your case," the judge said.

"Thank you, your honor."

The judge looked down at the docket. "Ah, the Costco case. You are charged with assault with a deadly weapon. Will, I need you to tell me, in your words, what happened that day."

Will went into his explanation, doing it as well as he could, following the advice from the sheriff. The judge asked Will a few questions and made several notes. He then asked Will to stand up.

"Will, based on your testimony and the testimony of those at the scene, I find you not guilty on the charge of assault with a deadly weapon. You are lucky that the dependant was not killed or we would be having a different discussion," the judge said. He picked up his gavel and hammered the desk.

Will shook for a moment. It was a wave of relief. Part of him was certain he was going to face some true justice. He had, after all, shot a man in broad daylight.

The sheriff grabbed Will's hand and shook it. "Congratulations," he said.

"Yeah, thanks," Will replied, feeling a touch lightheaded.

The sheriff shook the judge's hand as well. "Thanks."

"The facts determined the judgment here. Will has no criminal past. The defendant had a checkered past and provoked the incident."

"Well, no matter, the result is good. We are going to need all our patriots. We both know what's coming," the sheriff smiled.

The judge smiled, nodded, and then coughed harshly. Several people casually stepped back.

"Come on, Will, let's get you back home," the sheriff said.

Will shook the judge's hand again and followed the sheriff out the door and back to the squad car. When they arrived at the car, the deputy smiled at Will, seemingly knowing that things had gone well.

The sheriff drove Will back to his house. Will was quiet as they drove. The sheriff and his deputy were caught up in various case discussions. Will watched the landscape roll by, privately pleased he was still a free man.

As they rolled by houses, he noticed how many of them were boarded up. He also noticed there were still bodies wrapped up and awaiting transport to the burn site. His neighborhood was an older one. There had been a lot of deaths in the early days but they had leveled off in the last couple of weeks or so.

It was hard not to see that there was something serious happening to the world. His question, like those around him, was what was causing it. None of them believed that Covid was the cause. They knew it was the government behind what was happening. He struggled, though, to understand why any government would want to do that.

When they arrived back at Will's house, the sheriff got out of the car and let Will out of the back of the car. He then took Will's guns out of the trunk and handed them back to Will. Will fumbled a little holding his weapons.

"Now, Will, pardon the pun, but you dodged a bullet on this one. How about keeping those guns locked up unless you are on duty?"

"Yes, sir," Will replied, still struggling with the guns a little.

The sheriff nodded to him and got back in the car and drove off.

Will managed to get himself and his guns safely in the house.

He grinned a little. He had shot a man, in broad daylight, and was free. He was really taking a liking to his new world.

Riding the Rails

The train chugged along quietly as Jimmy lay in the darkness. He was glad he was in a mattress box. He wondered how Big Al was faring in his box. He suspected not so good.

The ride gave him time to think. The darkness slanted his thoughts. Once again he was caught in memories of his youth, in particular, those times when the decisions ultimately crafted his path in life.

It all seemed so innocent back then. He was young; he could change paths anytime he told himself, back then. The problem, in time, became while change was possible, it also had to be desired. In his case, the desire was simply never there.

He thought back to specific events and how, in the end, it only took a few bad decisions to place him in that box, on that train.

Jimmy shuffled positions. It was going to be a long ride and he needed to keep it together.

He found one that worked and he closed his eyes again and let the rhythm of the train carry him off to sleep.

It wasn't long before a dream came over him. He was standing on the rails just outside the freight car. It was dark outside, very dark. There were no stars in the sky. Something, in the dream, seemed very off to Jimmy.

He looked back into the freight car. There were a bunch of torn-up boxes but no people. He looked up and down both ends, nothing.

He turned and looked off into the distance when a light shining up toward the sky caught his eye. He looked around and could see nothing was moving, no cars, no people, nothing.

He decided his best bet was to head toward the light. He set out across a grassy field very cautiously. Following the light, Jimmy soon found himself standing in front of an old church. It was a small church, run-down, a typically rural one. It appeared to be abandoned.

Jimmy was unsure as to what to do next when the church doors opened. Someone stood in them. It was a man, all dressed in dark gray. He had stepped out the front doors and stood holding one of the doors open.

"Hello, Jimmy, we're glad you could join us," the gray man said.

Jimmy was taken aback by the man. Initially, it was the fact that he seemed to know Jimmy, but it was also the man's mannerisms and form.

"How do you know me?" Jimmy asked.

"I know everyone, Jimmy," he laughed.

The gray man waved his arm, inviting Jimmy into the church. "Come, join us. That is why you are here, isn't it?"

Jimmy looked around. There was darkness everywhere except in the church. He might have been a tough guy but he knew when the odds were against him. He started slowly walking toward the church doors.

He walked past the gray man, who held the door. Jimmy looked up and was amazed at how tall the man was.

Once inside the church, he could see where the light was coming from. There was a large bonfire burning on the altar. The roof of the church was gone. Whether it had burned off or some other foul end came to it, Jimmy didn't know, nor did he care.

He heard the doors slam behind him. He turned to see them close and also to see that the gray man was gone. He turned back to the altar.

A priest stood in front of the altar and the bonfire. He held a baby above a baptismal basin. He raised the baby high up and yelled, "Lord praise the purebloods."

The priest then slit the baby's throat with a straight razor and let the blood drain from the struggling body into the basin. When blood stopped running, the priest tossed the baby's carcass into the bonfire on the altar.

"Come feed, and be cleansed of this virus!" he exclaimed.

People scampered from under the church pews and hustled to the basin. They madly scooped at the blood in the basin and pulled it to their mouths.

"Drink, drink of the pure blood," the priest screamed as he turned and stared directly into Jimmy's eyes.

"Fucking hell," Jimmy muttered.

The train jostled roughly and Jimmy woke up. He then heard the unmistakable sounds of dogs.

Running the Gauntlet

Bobby was shaken awake.

"Hey, hey, what is it?" Bobby asked.

"We gotta go quiet. We got some company coming up on the starboard side," Jerome said quietly.

"Can't we just outrun them?"

"Yes, but depending on who they are, we could have problems further down the line. Our best bet is to be good and move on. That means we gonna have to hide you three. We all got yellow pass IDs, you three don't. That will be a problem."

Bobby sat up and looked around the bridge. "Yeah, of course, no problem."

"Merv will take you down below deck. We have a hiding spot. I would explain it tonight but we don't have time. I need to get you and the two girls in there now."

Bobby, recognizing the near panic in Jerome, quickly got up and followed Merv down into the galley. When they got there, he found the scene he had been avoiding. Sasha was lying, sleeping up against Sarah's body.

"Hey, dude, I'm real sorry, man," Merv said as they both stood paralyzed looking down at the two girls.

"I know. Thank you."

Bobby bent over and gently woke Sasha. "Honey, I'm sorry but we need to hide."

Sasha sat up, looked at Sarah, rubbed her eyes, and said, "Okay."

Merv opened a hatchway to the engine room. "We should put Sarah in first."

"Yes, makes sense," Bobby said and put his hands around her shoulders. Merv grabbed her feet and together they carefully slid her through the hatch.

Merv went through the hatch and opened a wall panel that had no marking. He waved Bobby in.

"We will hide her behind this panel. You and Sasha will be behind a panel on the other side of the engine room," Merv said.

Bobby looked around and connected the dots. He had always wondered where Jerome's wealth had come from. He had been told it was from smart investments. It seemed that the smart investment was a boat that could carry high-value products across the Gulf.

Merv noticed Bobby's look. "Brother, you need to stay quiet about this."

"Yeah, no worries."

Once Sarah was placed inside the panel, Merv put the cover back on. They waved Sasha in and moved over to the other side. Merv took two panel covers off. Sasha climbed into one compartment and Bobby into the other.

"Before you ask, there is an air vent and a small light in each compartment. You shouldn't have to be in there too long, maybe fifteen minutes or so, max," Merv said and then closed the panels.

Bobby lay back, wondering how many other people had been in that compartment over the years.

In the end, he and Sasha were in there for some twenty minutes. At one point, they heard the hatch to the engine room open up but no one came into the room. The hidden panel seemed to do the trick.

Jerome opened Bobby's panel this time.

"Nice investment," Bobby said as he climbed out.

"It just saved your ass."

"True."

Jerome opened up Sasha's panel and helped her out as well.

"Uncle Jerome, why do you have these hiding places?" Sasha smartly inquired.

Jerome smiled, squeezed one of her cheeks, and said, "The boat just came with them."

She smiled, "That's lucky. What about Sarah?"

"I think it would be best to leave her here for now," Jerome said.

"Aww, okay."

The group all headed back up to the bridge.

"So, what patrol was it?" Bobby asked.

"It was a coast guard patrol, legitimate. Those ones are not too bad right now. They just check the paperwork and do a quick walk-through. It's the bloody militia groups that are the real problem. These guys are trying to push everyone around. There have been some battles between the coast guard and those yahoos," Jerome replied.

Bobby looked out across the dark horizon. "How much longer?"

"A couple of hours, assuming no more interruptions. There is one more choke point, at Sabine Pass. It's a weird one right now. Half the waterway is Texas and half the waterway is in Louisiana. There are multiple patrols, from both states and various local militias. We're gonna need to get you back into the hold when we get there."

"No problem. It's quite comfy in there," Bobby smiled.

Jerome gave him a don't-go-there look.

Bobby and Sasha sat on the couch behind Jerome as he drove and enjoyed the warm late-fall air blowing through their hair. What was even better was the lack of the smell of the nightly body burns.

After a strangely enjoyable stretch, Jerome informed Bobby and Sasha that they needed to get back into their hidings. Once again Merv led them back down to the galley. Just before they went below deck, Bobby caught a glimpse of what he figured was the choke point. Boats could be seen circling all around the opening. There were towers installed on both sides of the shore with large spotlights. The whole thing reminded him of a scene out of *Apocalypse Now*, something he never dreamed possible in America.

At the sound of a gunshot, they all hustled to the engine room. Merv got them into the hidden compartments. As they got in, Bobby could not help noticing the smell of decay, of death. The smell had become commonplace in their lives but this was different, this was family, this was the smell of his daughter decaying.

He was happy to get into the closed-off compartment, away from the smell and the guilt. Once inside, he curled up into the fetal position and gently rocked back and forth.

He felt the boat glide to a stop again. Once again he could hear the footsteps of those who had come on board. This time the crew made their way down and into the engine.

Bobby could hear the conversation.

"For such a clean engine room, why does it smell like this?" someone asked.

"Ah, you caught us. We grabbed a few big fish while we were out. Figure we might be over the limit so we hide a couple in here," Jerome replied.

"Fish, huh. Where are they now?" a voice asked.

"We stuffed them in the galley freezer once we thought we were clear. Come on, I'll grab you guys one each."

"Alright, show us that freezer."

Bobby heard the engine room hatch close again.

He let out a sigh. He lay back and let himself relax. He thought of Sasha and how well she had been handling the situation. She had lost her mother, her grandfather, and her sister, right in front of her. Somehow she was holding it together, more so than Bobby would have imagined.

As he started to drift off into thought, he felt the boat accelerate quickly. The force pushed him back against the wall of the compartment. He could feel the boat swaying from port to starboard. He also heard what sounded like a gunshot. He covered his ears and began to hum to himself.

After some ten minutes, the compartment panel opened and Jerome stood in the opening.

"Shit, Jerome, what's going on out there?" Bobby asked, climbing out of the compartment.

"We had a little excitement. We got through the coast guard at the entry point with the fish trick but as soon as we got into the Sabine Pass we got the local militia assholes after us."

"I guess we got away," Bobby said.

"Of course we did. Those little shits are running fishing boats. The Gulf Legion, she's packing two world-class diesel engines. We left them bitches in our smoke," Jerome laughed.

Merv opened Sasha's compartment and helped her out.

"Come on, you two, let's head up top. The rest of the route should be clear sailing," Jerome said.

Bobby smiled, "After you, Captain."

Bobby reached back and grabbed Sasha's hand.

The four of them made their way up to the bridge. It was early afternoon and the late-fall sun was shining brightly.

Bobby and Sasha grabbed the little couch behind the pilot chair and Jerome relieved the driver. The raft driver and Merv took watchpoints with rifles in hand.

The sun's rays landed on Bobby and Sasha. She slid up against Bobby, hugging him, and for the first time in a while, Bobby felt relaxed.

Jerome turned around and smiled at them. "We'll be home soon."

Bobby smiled back and looked down at Sasha. She was asleep. She was also his last remaining family member; he knew he would do anything to save her.

A New Assignment

As soon as Will had packed his guns away, he gave Carlos a call.

"Carlos, good news, the judge found me not guilty!" he said.

"Shit, buddy, that is good news. I told you, sometimes you just gotta come clean with stuff."

Come clean, Will thought, good advice.

"I'm just happy it's over."

"Hey, I guess you are good for duty tonight," Carlos said.

"Yeah, I guess so. I think maybe I should call the lead and let him know."

"Good idea. Let me know after."

"Will do," Will replied and hung up.

Next, he dialed his shift lead's number.

"Hi, Bob, it's Will. I saw the judge today and he found me not guilty."

"That's great news, Will."

"I was wondering if I could come back on duty tonight?"

"Will, we talked about that at today's meeting. We decided that if the judge cleared you, we would have you back on duty but we think we should put you at another post."

Will wasn't sure what to think of that. He had been prepared for both a yes and a no, but not this. He did, however, quickly realize that a change was not so bad..

"Sure, I'm good with that."

"Good, that's what we need, Will. We're going to move you over to the east side, Chambers' line. It's likely going to be a little less hectic over there."

"Hmmm, I guess that makes sense."

"It does, Will. You shot a man."

That was true, Will had to concede. The ad hoc not-guilty verdict might have taken any criminal responsibility away; it did not, however, remove the reality of what he had done that day.

"Yes, I know."

"I'll text you the address. You can start tonight if you want, midnight shift."

"Is it possible that Carlos works with me? I mean, I'm his ride every night and all, and, well, we started together," Will asked.

There was a pause at the other end.

"I guess if Carlos is good with it. You gotta check with him and let me know. You gotta do it soon as we gotta update the roster for tonight."

"Yes, I'll call him right now."

"Alright, call me back once you've talked to him."

"Yes, I will," Will said and hung up.

He smiled. If he was to be taken off the front line, at least he could still be with Carlos, or at least he hoped he would be.

Will dialed another number, one that gave him an odd pleasure.

"Hey, Will. What's going on?" Carlos replied.

Hearing the voice, Will smiled to himself. "Well, I'm back on duty but they want to move to a new post, over on the east side."

"Geez, Will, does that mean we won't be working together anymore?"

Will smiled. That was exactly what he was hoping to hear.

"No, they told me if you want to come with me, that's up to you. What do you think?" Will asked hopefully.

"Hell, shit yeah, I'll come with you."

Will smiled ear to ear.

"Okay, let's meet at the bar, 7 pm?"

"For sure, I'll see you there."

Will hung up and glided euphorically into the kitchen to make himself a late lunch.

Preparing for D Day

The president stood looking out over the White House gardens when Jim came in to join him.

"It's time, sir," Jim said.

"I know. I'm just capturing this last moment of the America we've known," the president replied somberly.

"It is difficult times, sir."

"I imagine it's inappropriate to wish this had not happened on our shift."

"I'm sure all who live to see such times do. But that is not for them to decide. All we have to decide is what to do with the time that is given us," Jim smiled.

The president looked at Jim. "Thanks, Gandalf," he grinned.

"Well, things worked out for them in *Lord of the Rings*; they will work out for us."

The president put his hand on Jim's shoulder. "Come on, let's go face our fate."

With Jim leading the way, the two of them headed to the war room. When they got there, the rest of the team was waiting. It was a mix of politicians, military and civilian leaders.

"Are we ready for the new America?" the president asked.

"Yes sir," they replied.

"Alright, Jim, walk us through the plan one last time."

"Yes, sir. At exactly 6 pm this evening all media channels will be shut down. At the same time, all nuclear codes will be disabled and reprogrammed. All social platforms will be blocked including email platforms. A written message, from the president, will replace the landing pages on the internet as well as the media broadcast channels. The message will be simple. It will indicate that the president, as a result of the increasing pandemic and social unrest, is declaring a national state of emergency and martial law. They will be told that a night-time curfew is now in effect and the military has been deployed in every region of the country. Finally, it will be announced that the president will address the country at 7 pm."

"Adam, where do we stand on the military deployment?" the president asked.

"The first wave deployed to strategic positions overnight last night. They will take the target posts this evening and night. The first wave will target the hot spots where the militia is the most dangerous. We will neutralize those positions and establish a new borderline. The goal is overwhelming force and to leverage our advantage in technology," the Joint Chief of Staff replied.

"And casualties?"

"We have estimated approximately 3,500 to 4,000 first wave, 80% militia, 20% military."

"Jesus," the president said.

"Mr. President, we are losing some 20,000 or more a day from Omega as a comparison," the chief medical officer said.

"Neither number is good, but this is why we are here. Jane, are we ready on the media side?"

"Everything is ready to go based on the plan Jim outlined," the head of the FCC replied.

"Jim, I assume we are all set for 7 pm," the president said.

"Yes, you received the speech last night. We have the media team set up in the Oval Office. As Jane indicated, the internet and broadcast channels are ready to go. Your speech will be live-fed on all broadcast channels and social media platforms. Following that, it will be rerun every hour for the next forty-eight hours."

"The last stage will be dealing with those who want to join the new America from the red zones. Where are we with establishing transfer points?" the president asked.

"Once the military safely has control of the border points, we, in conjunction with Homeland Security, will establish intake facilities."

"Just for clarification, everyone is still an American citizen, correct?" someone asked.

"Yes, they are. What we have done is to establish regional health boundaries with entry rules. This allows us to control access within the greater American territory. We are not redrawing the legal lines of America, we are redrawing the movement boundaries, at least for now," the head of Homeland Security replied.

Everyone in the room knew that was the headline. The real truth was it was very likely the first step toward a segregated America. What was happening in America was more than a virus. The cracks in the seams of the country ran deeper than that and had been brewing long before Covid was a household name.

"There is also the foreign policy matter. We will be making a statement to the U.N. about the actions we are taking. The statement will be consistent with what we have discussed here. It is important that the world see this as an internal issue, managing the virus risk," the Secretary of State said.

"Any more questions?" the president asked.

"Yes, any feedback from the GOP?" the Speaker asked.

"No, nothing of any value. It seems they are willing to play a waiting game. Frankly, once we execute this plan, we'll hear from them and on our terms," the president replied.

"I certainly hope they do. The country is better off united," the House Minority Leader replied.

"Are there any more questions?" the president asked.

No one replied.

"Alright, I know this is a very challenging moment for all of us. I, likely as most of you, haven't slept for nights now. We all have jobs to do. May God help us," the president said, once again, still unsure if he believed in God anymore.

The End of the Line

Jimmy lay as still and quiet as he could. The train had stopped. He had dealt with dogs in the past, police service dogs specifically. He knew how effective they could be.

The dogs came so close to Jimmy's box he could hear them sniffing. He held his breath until the sound went away. Whatever they had sprayed them with seemed to have done the trick. He hoped the rest of them were able to hold their own as well.

As he lay quiet, he reflected on the dream he had just had. He was never much of a dreamer. Why that was? He never knew. His sleep was generally dark, void of thought, blank in many ways. Some days he would awaken surprised at life, almost as if he was a newborn. Often, he wished he was, with a chance to start over and make different decisions along the way.

The train lunged forward again and Jimmy breathed a sigh of relief. He was one step closer to salvation, even if he didn't necessarily believe he was worthy of it.

He closed his eyes again and waited for what was to come next.

A couple of hours later, the train creaked to a stop again. Jimmy rolled over onto his stomach, prepared for action if need be. He heard footsteps and held his breath. There was a knocking on his box.

"Yo, Jimmy, it's DeSantos. We're here."

Jimmy let his breath out. The box was torn open and the wooden frame lifted. Jimmy stood up and stepped out into the freight car. Big Al was there, stretching his back.

"Hey, Big Al, you're not looking too good," Jimmy said jokingly.

"My fucking back. You got a bed. I got stuck on a damn chair," he moaned.

DeSantos chuckled a little in the background. He tossed a can of beer to each Jimmy and Big Al.

"Sit down and have a beer, you two, while we get the rest of the group out," he said.

Jimmy and Big Al grabbed a box to sit on and opened their beers.

"Where do you think we are?" Jimmy asked Big Al between swigs of beer.

"I hope near the damn border. Did you hear them dogs come on?"

"Yeah, nearly pissed myself. I don't do too good with dogs."

"Me either. Shit man, it don't matter now we're here."

"Yup, wherever here is."

DeSantos returned with the rest of the crew, all looking as rough as Big Al did.

"Congrats, folks, you've made it to the last stage. It's 11 pm. We're going to leave the train now and head to another safe house. It's about an hour's walk. We'll spend the rest of the night and day there. Once it's dark again we gonna have another nice walk, this one down to the waterfront where we gonna meet a boat. We are in a green zone now but we still have to be careful cause we don't have the proper documentation or passport," DeSantos announced.

The crew all threw their packs on and followed him back out into the dark night.

A Reprieve from the Storm

After a long, trying night and day, Jerome's boat pulled up to the dock at the back of his home along Sabine Lake.

Once the boat was secure, Jerome guided Bobby and Sasha off the boat and onto the dock.

"Let's get Sasha inside and settled and we'll come back for Sarah," Jerome said.

"Thank you."

They walked through the rear doors and were greeted by Jerome's wife, Cecilia. She immediately hugged Bobby. "I'm so sorry," she whispered.

She then took hold of Sasha's hand and led her to the kitchen. "Come on, my dear, let's get you fed."

"Thanks again, Jerome," Bobby said.

"No problem. I wish we had been able to get to you earlier. Since this is a yellow zone, we don't see the worst of what is going on out there and, to be honest, this stretch here along the waterfront is well insulated from the shit out there. I pretty much gave up on the news as it's just politics at this point."

"I'm starting to realize just how much of this whole damn thing is political now that I've lost half my family."

"Shit, man, I really am sorry. I suggest we go get Sarah."

"Yes, please."

The two of them headed back out to the boat. As they walked along the side of the boat, Bobby noticed a hole in the side.

"Jerome," Bobby said and pointed.

"Shit. Bloody bullet hole. It's those damn militia groups."

"Well, at least it's only the boat that got hit."

The three of them looked briefly at the hole; it seemed to fit about a 9 mm bullet.

"Come on," Jerome said.

They boarded the boat and headed down to the engine room. Once they opened the hatch, the odor was noticeably stronger.

"Jerome, we'll need to bury her."

"Yes, we will. I have a large freezer in the garage we can store her for now."

With no further words spoken, they removed the panel and gently carried Sarah's stiff body up to the garage.

They quietly laid her body down while Jerome cleared out some room. Bobby looked down at Sarah's form, wrapped up in blankets, laying there. He sat down on the floor and began to cry.

Jerome grabbed him by the arm and helped him back up onto his feet. "Come on, big guy, you have another daughter who needs you."

"Yeah, you're right," Bobby replied, straightening himself up.

The two of them lifted Sarah's body and placed it into the freezer.

Jerome put his arm around Bobby's shoulder. "Come on, let's go join the rest of the family."

They headed back into the house and made their way into the kitchen where they found Sasha sitting with Cecilia.

"Daddy, Aunt Cecilia makes the best chicken!" Sasha exclaimed with her mouth half full.

Bobby smiled. It was nice to see Sasha happy. Cecilia was a good woman and would have made a brilliant mother, in Bobby's opinion, had she and Jerome ever had children. He had asked Jerome once about it; the reaction was enough for him to leave that story alone.

"Let me get you two some food," Cecilia said.

"Thank you, Cecilia," Bobby smiled.

"Uncle Jerome, I love your house," Sasha said between bites.

"Well, we love having you here."

Cecilia gave them each a plate of food and a beer. "Come on Sasha, we've got a brand new, really big TV."

"Oh, wow, really?"

"Yes, really. Come on, let's go see what's on."

Sasha jumped up and followed Cecilia out of the room.

"So, we are going to bury Sarah, right?" Bobby asked as he and Jerome sat at the table.

"Yes. We have a place nearby where we have been taking care of those who pass in the neighborhood. It's part of a local Baptist church that we belong to and there is a cemetery there. The pastor has been keeping space for us. Sarah will rest in a good place."

Bobby nodded. "Thank you."

Jerome put his hand on Bobby's. "Tonight, how about we just take a break?"

Bobby smiled at him. "Yeah, I could do that."

They finished their dinner quickly and quietly. "Come on, let's go join your daughter."

They headed into the large family room of Jerome's house to find Sasha curled up with Cecilia on a large, spectacular couch. For a moment, with the sunlight cutting across her, Bobby mistook Cecilia for Lilly.

Sasha looked up at her father. "Daddy, look at the TV!"

"It's a seventy-five inch, 4K TV for the record," Jerome said quietly.

Bobby went and sat down on the couch. Sasha kissed Cecilia and slid over beside Bobby. He put his arm around her and felt her warmth creep up onto him. Within minutes, he was deep into a much-needed sleep.

D Day

Everything was in place, or so the president was told. There were times in his presidency when he might have questioned what he was told. He no longer had that luxury. He was, as they say, all in at this point.

He sat at his desk in the Oval Office looking up at the camera, gathering his internal fortitude and trying not to sweat through the makeup.

"Mr. President, you're on," the media lead said and pointed straight at him.

It was showtime. The biggest show time of his lifetime.

He knew the speech inside out. He had been reading and re-reading the damn thing for some twenty-four straight hours. He knew every word, every syllable of it by heart. He needed to; it was perhaps the most important presidential speech since the Gettysburg Address.

"Good evening, my fellow Americans," the president started and went into his speech.

The lights went off and he breathed a sigh of relief. He nearly collapsed but somehow managed to hold on. Jim and the team cleared the camera crew and all non-essential people out of the Oval Office.

'Excellent Job, Sir," Jim said once the room the empty.

"Jim, I could use a good Scotch."

"I can get that for you, sir. However, we have Matt and the GOP on the line. They are asking to speak with you."

"Tell them I'll call them back. They had their chance to speak; they made the wrong decision."

"Yes, sir. Let me get you that Scotch."

A DIY Funeral

Bobby woke on a comfortable bed in one of the many spare rooms in Jerome's house. While he wasn't entirely sure how he had gotten there, he knew it was innocent enough.

He got himself dressed and went to find Sasha. As it turned out, finding Sasha was simple enough. She was planted on the couch, back in the family room, with Cecilia and Jerome.

"Daddy, come, have pancakes with us," she smiled.

Bobby smiled. Sasha had been a trooper; she had earned a reprieve from the hell that world had become.

"Alright, Sasha, I'm in."

Cecilia got up and motioned to Bobby. "Sit, please. You are our guest."

Bobby nodded and sat down with Sasha. He grabbed one of Sasha's pancakes and shoved it into his mouth.

"Hey," she yelled at him.

Bobby smiled and Sasha smiled back. It was a bright moment, an odd one albeit, in what had become a dark tale.

Cecilia popped back in with a fresh stack of pancakes.

"Yeah, Aunt Cecilia!" Sasha exclaimed.

Sasha, Bobby, and Jerome all dug in.

Once they had all eaten their fill, Jerome casually pulled Bobby aside.

"We need to head over to the church and make the arrangements for later today," Jerome said.

"Yes, we do. Thank you, by the way."

"All right, get cleaned up and we'll head out shortly. Cecilia will take Sasha over to one of our friend's houses. They have a daughter, roughly the same age as her. We've lost a lot of people around here, maybe not as many as in those red zones, your red zone, Bobby, but more than folks here are used to and they're feeling the pain just like everyone else is," Jerome said.

Bobby was momentarily caught off guard. The last four days had been a horror for him and Sasha. Yes, it had become about them, for a reason, but in reality, the world was fucked for everyone, just to varying degrees.

Bobby smiled. In some ways, keeping up the impression of normality gave people an excuse to pretend life was as it had always been, even when it wasn't.

He slipped back to his room, showered, and got changed. He headed down to the kitchen where he found Jerome and Merv.

"Ready?" Jerome asked.

"Yup, let's go."

The three of them headed out to the garage. There were three cars in there. A Porsche, a Corvette, and a Hummer.

"We'll take the Hummer," Jerome said.

Bobby gave him a look.

"We all have our businesses, Bobby," Jerome said.

"Apparently, some are better than others," Bobby said as he climbed up into the Hummer.

They all settled in and Jerome drove them out of the garage.

"Last night you said that there have been a lot of losses here. I'm assuming you mean deaths," Bobby said as they drove.

"Yeah, you will see what I mean when we get to the church. Whatever this thing is, it's bad," Jerome replied.

"Yo, Bobby, are you vaccinated?" Merv asked from the back seat.

"No. What about you guys?"

"I'm right up-to-date," Merv replied.

"I got three of them. Trying to get the super booster for Cecilia and I."

The car stopped at a light. Jerome turned and looked directly at Bobby.

"Is Sasha vaccinated?"

"No."

"Jesus, Bobby. Why not? This thing is a death sentence. You know that better than anyone. We need to get her covered. Once we get Sarah's funeral done, we're gonna find Sasha the vaccines she needs."

Bobby nodded. He knew Jerome was right. In reality, he had known for a long time. He allowed himself to be bullied into making decisions that cost him his daughter and his wife. The anger at his father continued to grow in him.

As they drove, Bobby could tell the neighborhood was wealthy. It had all the tell tale signs. He wondered how many of them were legitimate and how many were gangsters, so to speak. In the end, it didn't seem to matter; they all shared the same space.

They pulled into the parking lot of the church. For a Baptist church, it was quite upscale. It was not a surprise to Bobby, given the rest of the neighborhood.

"Come on, let's go talk to the pastor," said Jerome.

Inside the church, Bobby was even more impressed. The place reeked of wealth. It seemed it was a good spot to be a Baptist minister.

"Ah, Jerome, what a pleasure to see you again," the minister said and reached his hand out.

Jerome smiled and shook the man's hand.

"Minister Joseph, it is a pleasure to see you as well. We have come with a request. This is my cousin, Bobby. His daughter recently died, and we would like the honor to bury her here, in this cemetery," Jerome said politely.

The minister looked over at Bobby. "Was she a member of our congregation?"

Great, Bobby thought, *just one more problem.*

"No, she wasn't, minister. However, I'm happy to provide a donation to the church in lieu," Jerome replied.

"Donations are always appreciated, Jerome. I must note, however, that with the times we are living in, our cemetery, as you can appreciate, is running tight."

Jerome grinned at the minister. It wasn't a casual, pleasant grin between friends. There was nothing pleasant about it. The grin was uncomfortable for everyone there and it seemed to have the intended effect on the minister.

"Of course, given your status in the community, I'm sure we can accommodate your family," the minister said with a forced smile.

Jerome shook the minister's hand. Bobby did as well. "Thank you," Bobby said.

"Jerome, I have other business to attend, so please, see Keith in the yard. He will work with you to find an appropriate spot," Minister Joseph said.

"Thank you, again," Bobby said.

The minister smiled and left.

"Come on, Bobby, let's go find Keith," Jerome said as he grabbed Bobby by the shoulder.

Merv laughed. "Shit, You gonna love this guy."

They headed back out of the church and around to the rear.

"Hey, Jerome, what was up with the donation thing?" Bobby asked as they walked.

"What do you think pays for this place?" Jerome laughed.

"I can help up, with the money, I mean," Bobby said.

"God, no, don't worry about it. I'm just happy to help out."

Bobby was good with that answer. He had no idea what the price tag on a donation was, but having seen the neighborhood and the church, he was pretty sure it was out of his range.

They found a small building behind the church and Jerome knocked on the door. An elderly man with a slight hunch answered the door.

"Ah, Mr. Jerome. How can I help you?" the man asked with an eastern European accent.

"Minister Joseph asked us to speak with you, Keith, about a burial plot, for my niece."

"For your niece? The minister approved this?"

"Yes, he did."

Keith looked at the three of them. Bobby noticed that his face was somewhat disfigured in places and there was something off about his eyes.

"Alright, come with me."

The three men followed Keith out to a four-seater golf cart. Keith got in and waved the other three in. They drove out into the cemetery.

The first thing that struck Bobby was the number of fresh graves.

"Bobby, I think you can see what I was saying about the deaths here. It's not what you would have seen back home but for our community, it is huge," Jerome turned and said.

Bobby said nothing. He just watched as the cart rolled past new grave after new grave. The volume surprised Bobby. It was a visual representation of the pain the virus was inflicting on humanity.

Bobby knew the numbers were worse where he came from but they were mostly hiding in the smell of the nightly burns. Here, the count was clear in each new hole in the ground.

They reached the back area of the cemetery where the last remaining sacred ground remained, and Keith stopped the cart.

He got out and looked at Bobby. "How old was your daughter?"

"Hum, eleven, she was just eleven years old," Bobby replied.

Keith continued to look at Bobby awkwardly. He then began to hum something. He stopped and walked toward a spot near the back.

"This area will do. It is where we are putting the kids now."

While the three men stood looking at the ground, Keith walked back to the cart and opened the trunk area on the back. He pulled out three shovels and tossed them on the ground.

"If you want a burial, you had best start digging," he said and walked to a specific spot on the grass. He took out a can of spray paint and outlined a rectangle in orange against the late-fall grass.

He returned to the cart and sat down. "If you want that burial today, you better all get digging," he said and took a cigarette out.

Bobby looked at Jerome. Jerome stepped over to the shovels and picked one up. "Well, guys, we got work to do," he said and started to dig.

Bobby and Merv grabbed the other two shovels and joined in.

A Faulty Safe House

Jimmy, Big Al, and crew walked under the cover of darkness for well over an hour before they reached the safe house. The house wasn't much more than a shack in a wooded area somewhere at the end of the line in northwestern New York state.

The crew had lost much of the enthusiasm it had started with that night in the bar. It had been sucked away by the hardships of the journey and the growing reality of the risk they were undertaking.

As they filed into the small, rustic, musty living room, Jimmy and likely every other member of the crew could not help but notice the crosses and faded pictures of Jesus spread across the peeling walls.

"Jesus," Big Al muttered.

"You can say that again," one of the crew replied.

An older woman walked into the room. "Hello everyone, I'm Taren Hoops and this is my home. Well, I share it with Jesus."

There was a little chuckling, following her introduction.

"What's so funny? If any of you are unbelievers, there is the door!" she screamed.

"Ah, no, no, we're all believers," Big Al replied.

She smiled again. "Good. You all wait here. I'm making tea," she said and left the room again.

"I guess I should have told you all, Taren is a bit of a nut job. Just stay quiet about any of the Jesus shit," DeSantos said quietly.

Some of the guys grabbed a seat where they could. The room was smaller than it had been at the previous safe house so even though there were fewer of them than there was previously, Jimmy and Big Al found themselves standing.

As they waited, they could hear Taren coughing away in the kitchen.

"I ain't drinking any of that tea," Big Al whispered to Jimmy.

Jimmy knew he was not touching anything that crazy women put in front of him. He was going to do his time for the day and as soon as they were clear to hit the road, he'd be out of there like a shot.

Taren returned carrying a tray full of mismatched teacups. She placed the tray on the small wooden table in the middle of the room.

"Please, everyone, take a cup," she said, eyeing the group.

"I'd prefer a beer," one of the guys replied.

Taren turned and shot a glance at the man. "We do not serve the devil's juice in here," she screamed at him.

He hesitantly reached over and took a teacup. Everyone else took a cup as well.

Jimmy noticed that a couple of the guys took sips of the tea.

"Taren, a few crackers would go well with this tea," DeSantos said.

"Yes, it would. I have some in the kitchen. I'll grab them."

As soon as she left the room, DeSantos poured most of his tea into a plant pot. He waved to the rest of them to do the same. Jimmy and Big Al poured theirs into a tall plant near the front door.

Taren returned a few moments later with a second tray filled with crackers and small cookies.

Some of the guys grabbed a few crackers and cookies.

Jimmy and Big Al passed on them.

"Now, I know you folks have been traveling and are likely tired so once you finish your tea, we have two rooms for you all. They have bunk beds, so four per room. I have to go to the church now; there is a lot to do," Taren said and headed down the hallway.

DeSantos got up, grabbed the girl that had shown up on the train, and headed over to Jimmy and Big Al.

"Guys, follow me. I want you two in our room," DeSantos said.

The two of them immediately followed him down the hallway and into one of the rooms. DeSantos closed and locked the door.

"Sorry, guys, but honestly I don't wanna be in a room with those other guys."

The comment surprised Jimmy, at least somewhat. He had expected someone running a gig like DeSantos would be neutral on those paying into it but there was a risk, lots of it, and he seemed pretty damn good at managing risk.

"Yo, DeSantos, what's up with that Taren chick?" Big Al asked as he settled in a bottom bunk.

"She's a piece of work. The place used to be run by a buddy of mine. He died two weeks ago, Omega. The chick is his mom. She owns this place now and yeah, she's wacked. We just gotta put up with her for a bit and then we out of here."

The girl, who appeared to be in her early twenties, climbed up onto the top bunk above DeSantos and lay down. No one said a word about her.

DeSantos took out a bottle of rum and a bag of cocaine. "Hey, we got some time to kill. You guys want a drink and a bump?"

This time, Jimmy did; he needed them. "Yeah, I'm in."

"Me too," Big Al said.

Nothing from the top bunk.

DeSantos put the cheap bottle of Puerto Rican rum on the table and rolled out a few lines.

The bottle passed back and forth between them for a couple of hours. As it did, the conversation opened more and more.

"Have you guys thought about life in Canada? I mean, we've been told it's different and better than it is here but what if it isn't?" Big Al asked.

It was a sensible question, one that should have been asked before money was handed over and they got in that tunnel. For Jimmy, it could not be any worse than the Barrio.

"It is better, I know. You're not the first group I've run up there. They got just about everyone vaccinated, with all four shots, before Omega hit. They don't have red zones, or any zones, they just got their world and it's a shitload better than ours," DeSantos replied, wiping cocaine residue from his nose.

"Damn, I hope so. I always wanted to visit Canada but never could cause of my criminal record," Big Al said.

"Yeah, me too. What about you, Jimmy?" DeSantos asked.

"I think anywhere is better than where we were."

Big Al laughed. "I'll drink to that," he said and took another swig from the rum bottle.

"Well, with that, I'm done," Jimmy said and climbed up to the bunk above Big Al's.

"Good idea, I'm checking out too," DeSantos said and crawled into the bottom bunk across the way.

Jimmy kept his clothes on. The sheets stank. He had no idea how many people had been in that bunk before him but after one look at crazy Taren, he knew he was best to be safe.

It wasn't long before the sounds of snoring enveloped the room.

Many hours into his sleep, Jimmy was awakened by pounding on the door. He quickly jumped down.

Big Al and DeSantos also jumped out of bed.

"What the fuck, man?" DeSantos said.

He opened the door and there stood Leon.

"Hey, I hate to do this, but Mickey is real sick. He's choking and spitting up blood and shit," Leon said.

"Fuck, man, what the hell do you want me to do about it? He's probably got fucking Omega. Keep him in his room," DeSantos yelled at him.

"What is going on?" a voice said from down the hall. It was Taren and she was quickly making her way toward them.

"Shit," DeSantos muttered.

"One of our crew is sick, real sick, ma'am," Leon said.

"Bring me to him," she demanded.

Leon walked back to the room with her.

"This ain't good," DeSantos muttered.

Taren emerged from the room and exclaimed, "This man has the devil in him. We must bring him to the church immediately."

With Taren leading, Leon, with help from Phil, dragged Mickey out of the room.

"Just hold still, guys," DeSantos whispered and held his arm out in front of Jimmy and Big Al.

Taren led them to the front door and then stopped. She looked back. "Where are the rest of you? You must all be cleansed," she yelled.

"Fuck," DeSantos whispered.

"You must come now or forever be dammed," Taren yelled down the hall.

She opened a closet and pulled out a shotgun. She cocked it.

"Come now!" she yelled.

"We're going to have to go. Just the three of us," he said, motioning to the girl on the top bunk.

"We're coming, Taren," DeSantos replied.

The three men put their coats on and followed a crazy woman out the front door to God knows what end.

A Funeral for a Princess

It took the three men about two hours to dig down the nearly six feet that Keith insisted they do. Once down, Keith drove them, all sweaty, back to the church parking lot.

"The minister will call you soon to arrange a time for later today. You need to bring the girl's body here as soon as you can. It needs to be prepared," Keith said and drove off in the cart.

The three guys got back into the Hummer.

"That guy is a barrel of laughs," Bobby said bitterly.

"I told you you would love him," Merv replied.

"Love ain't quite the word that comes to mind."

"Bobby, what kind of character would you expect to dig graves?" Jerome asked as he drove.

Bobby thought about it. "That one."

"Let's focus on having a proper funeral, one fit for your daughter."

"Yes, you're right, Jerome. This isn't about us. It's about her."

Jerome reached over and put his hand on Bobby's shoulder. "Exactly."

They arrived back home right around the lunch hour and found Cecilia with Sasha sitting out on the back deck in the sun enjoying a lunch.

"Ah, the men are back," Cecilia smiled.

"Daddy, why are you all sweaty?"

Bobby looked down at himself. He was covered in sweat as were the other two.

"It was really hot where we were."

"Oh, Daddy, that's just silly." She smiled and took another bite of her lunch.

Bobby walked over to her and kissed her on the head. "Don't worry, Jerome has plenty of showers here."

She smiled back.

Cecilia looked at Jerome. "I think all three of you need a good shower."

"Okay, okay, I know when I'm not wanted. Come on, guys, we need to get cleaned up."

The three of them headed into the house.

"She's right. Let's shower and properly dress. Once we do, Bobby, you and I need to bring Sarah down to the church."

"Yes, we do," Bobby replied. The situation was beginning to hit home. Her death that night wasn't the end; it was just the beginning of the end. Digging her grave, bringing her body to be prepared, and seeing her placed underground replayed the pain of that moment of death, again and again.

It was the *right* thing to do? It was the *honorable* thing to do, but for whom? His daughter was dead. What the hell did honor matter now?

He shook his thoughts off and headed for the shower.

A half-hour later, the men all met downstairs again.

"Merv, I think we are good with just Bobby and me for this one. How about you have a look at the bullet hole in the boat and see what we can do with that?" Jerome said.

"Yeah, sure, no problem. I think we might have taken a couple of bullets," Merv said and headed out to the dock.

"Come on, let's go get your daughter," Jerome said.

Bobby and Jerome headed down to the garage and the freezer.

"You ready?" Jerome asked.

"Yup."

Jerome opened the freezer. They both reached in and lifted Sarah out. Her body was completely frozen and hard.

They carried it out to the Hummer and placed it in the back.

They got in and headed off to the church.

"I'm sure you have some questions about my line of work at this point, Bobby?"

Bobby, looking out the window, replied, "In a different time, I would. Right now, I couldn't care less."

With that, the two drove in silence to the church. When they arrived, Jerome drove around to the back, to another building.

"This is the mortuary; this is where we need to drop Sarah off."

Jerome parked the Hummer and the two got out. They went into the mortuary and found it quite busy inside.

"Jesus, lots going on in here," Bobby said.

"Yup, like I said, we've had our share of dead."

Bobby did not doubt that. The world had had its share of death.

They waited patiently to meet with the attendant. When they finally did speak with him, they were told that there would be a graveside funeral at 5 pm that night.

"Graveside?" Jerome asked.

"Sir, the young woman was not a member of this church."

Before Jerome escalated the situation, Bobby stepped in.

"Jerome, that's fine. The last thing I want to do right now is sit in bloody church."

Jerome looked at Bobby closely. Bobby could see that Jerome understood. He turned back to the attendant.

"Alright, 5 pm is fine. Where do we bring the body?"

"Where is she now?"

"In the back of our truck. She is frozen."

"We will send a cart out for her. Wait by your vehicle."

Jerome thanked him and he and Bobby headed back to the Hummer.

"Sorry about the church, but I get you—I can't stand sitting through those things either. I'm still a little pissed that I had to pay for this after everything Cecilia does for this place."

"Well, that's religion for you."

After a couple of minutes' wait, a service cart pulled up behind the Hummer. Jerome and Bobby placed Sarah in the back of the cart. Bobby signed a couple of documents, and they were on their way back home.

"Sorry I got on you yesterday about the vaccines and shit," Jerome said.

"It's okay. You were right. We listened to my dad. Now he's dead, and Lilly and Sarah are dead."

"Sorry to say, but your dad was a complete ass."

"Yeah, I know."

"Alright, let's get home and get this thing organized."

When they arrived home, they found Cecilia, Sasha, and Merv out on the back deck.

"So, what is the plan, Jerome?" Cecilia asked.

"We have a graveside funeral at 5 pm."

"It's 2:30 now, so we will have to start getting ready in about an hour. We'll have to find a nice little dress for you, Sasha," Cecilia said.

"A dress." Sasha smiled.

"Yes, a pretty dress."

"For you, Bobby, you are about the same size as Merv. Merv, find something for Bobby, will you?" Jerome said.

"I got something in mind," Merv grinned.

"I'm not sure that's a good thing." Jerome smiled at Bobby.

Jerome got up and headed into the kitchen. He returned with a bottle of bourbon and placed it on the table with three glasses.

"I think it's time for a drink," he said.

The other two smiled.

Jerome poured them each a large glass and they all settled in.

"I think that's our call to leave, Sasha." Cecilia smiled.

The two girls headed into the house.

The sun was shining again and, as Bobby sipped his Tennessee bourbon, sitting on a deck, looking over the waterway, he could almost forget the hell his life had been over the past few weeks.

"Bobby, after the funeral, we need to get both of you up-to-date on the vaccines," Jerome said.

"I would appreciate that."

"For now, let's enjoy an hour of sunshine and some good bourbon." They clinked glasses.

"Right on," Merv replied

About an hour later, following several more glasses, Bobby reached the point where guilt was overcoming pleasure.

"While this has been a nice break, I think I need to get ready," he said.

"I think we all do, Bobby. Merv, why don't you take Bobby and show him what you got for him?"

"You got it, boss. Come on, Bobby."

Bobby followed Merv up to the room he kept in Jerome's house. The room was spectacular. It was a self-contained little space with a king bed, an entertainment setup, and small office space. In there, Merv showed him a walk-in closet full of clothes.

"Wow, you sure got a great setup here," Bobby said, looking around at the clothes.

"Yeah, thanks. Your cousin has been really good with me. I was gangbanger when our paths first crossed. He knew my momma and wanted to help so he brought me in working for him. Eventually, when my momma died, he brought me into his home. I love the man. I love both of them like family."

Bobby was learning a lot about his cousin. He had visited with Jerome a few times over the years, but they were never really close. If Bobby were being honest, he had always envied Jerome and was a touch jealous.

"He certainly seems to be a good man," Bobby replied somewhat subconsciously.

"Okay, here are a couple of outfits I had in mind," Merv said.

Merv took down two suits. The first looked like something right out of *Solid Gold*. Bobby laughed. Merv looked at him and said, "I kinda thought you might pass on this one."

He showed Bobby the second outfit. It was perfect. It was the kind of outfit that Lilly had always said Bobby would look good in. Maybe this was preordained, he thought, or maybe he was just hoping to find a connection to the woman, who, in the end, he had wronged.

"I like that," he finally said.

"It's yours now, brother," Merv replied and handed him the outfit.

"Thank you, this means a lot to me," Bobby replied and shook Merv's hand.

"Anytime."

Bobby headed back to his room. He put the outfit on his bed and looked down at it. For a moment, he was tempted to call Lilly, to let her know that he found something she would like.

It was that simple, at least it used to be. They called each other all the time for good things, bad things, or frankly anything just to catch each other's voices. That was the one thing Bobby missed the most. He could not count how many times since she had died that he had reached for his phone when a moment struck him, reaching for her.

He made his way to the bathroom, leaving the emotion laying back on the bed.

He showered and put the outfit on. He walked down to the kitchen to join the rest of the group.

"Damn, Bobby, you clean up good," Jerome said.

"You look wonderful, Bobby," Cecilia said.

Sasha ran over to Bobby and hugged him.

"Daddy, do you like my dress?" she asked.

"Of course, I do. You look beautiful."

"Do you think Mommy would like it?"

Bobby paused for the moment. Lilly was already fresh on his mind. Lilly loved both girls; they were her treasures. She wasn't one for education or career. She longed for family and got one, a beautiful one at that. Then one day, through no fault of her own, it was all torn away from her.

"Yes, she would, very much so, Sasha," Bobby replied, hiding a tear.

"We all ready to go?" Jerome asked.

They all headed to the garage, climbed into Jerome's Hummer, and headed back to the church.

"Hey, I didn't invite anyone else today. I kinda figure this is a private event," Jerome said quietly as they drove.

"Thanks. Yeah, it is very private."

It was private for Bobby. There was no way he wanted to expose the series of events that led up to this or worse, the decisions.

They pulled into what was a pretty full church parking lot.

"You folks wait here. I'll go let the minister know we're here," Jerome said.

"Daddy, that's a nice church," Sasha said.

"It sure is," Bobby replied, trying to forget the donation conversation with the minister.

A few moments later, Jerome popped back out of the church and hustled over to the Hummer.

He climbed in and said, "The minister is going to meet us over at the gravesite. He's pressed for time," Jerome said sarcastically.

The Omega Variant

They drove over to the grave they had dug earlier in the day. The drive was a touch challenging due to the amount of traffic in the cemetery.

"Daddy, why are there so many graves?"

Before Bobby could reply, Jerome jumped in.

"It's an old graveyard, Sasha, so it's had many years for graves to add up."

Bobby gave Jerome a quick thank-you nod.

After a few required maneuvers around the parked vehicles of other mourners, they pulled up on the grass right by the grave.

"Maybe the Hummer wasn't the best choice," Bobby said to Jerome.

"I think you might be right."

The five of them walked the last few steps to the gravesite.

Sasha grabbed her father's hand when they reached it. "Daddy, this is for Sarah?"

"Yes, it is."

"It's just like Mommy's."

"Yes, it is."

Bobby noticed Keith approaching on a cart. He had a trailer in tow behind him. Bobby was pretty sure what the trailer was carrying.

Bobby caught Jerome's attention. Jerome got it and headed over to cut Keith off at the pass.

On another cart, Bobby could see the minister coming.

"Come on, let's get ready," Bobby said to Cecilia, Sasha and Merv.

The four of them got themselves graveside. The hole was just as they had left it earlier in the day, except for a set of white straps across the top. There was, however, a simple headstone at the top of the grave. It read, 'Sarah Megan Jones. Born May 10, 2014, Died Nov 8, 2025.'

The sight of the words engraved in stone was a little bit too much for Bobby. He began to cry. Cecilia quickly put her arm around him.

"Daddy, don't cry. She's not sick anymore and she is with Mommy now," Sasha said.

The simplicity of a child, Bobby thought. He wished he had had that simplicity at the moment.

The minister came to join them and shook everyone's hand.

"Cecilia, it is truly wonderful to see you again," he said.

"It is lovely to see you again, Minister, however, I wish it were under better circumstances."

"We all do, child, in such times."

The minister headed to the top of the grave by the gravestone and took a Bible out.

Jerome walked back over to the grave. He grabbed Bobby and Merv. "Guys, we need to carry the coffin in."

The three of them headed over to the trailer. Keith was there with a large young man.

"This is Timmy. He's going to help you guys carry the coffin," Keith said.

"Alright then," Jerome said, looking up at the big man.

"You best be doing it now. We got a real busy schedule today," Timmy said.

Timmy guided the other three men to the back of the trailer. "We gonna slide the coffin out of the trailer. Two men on each side. It ain't as heavy as a typical coffin cause it's one for a kid, so the four of us should be good with it."

Timmy and Bobby took one side while Jerome and Merv took the other. Timmy reached in and pulled the small coffin forward. As it slid out of the trailer, each man grabbed a handle.

It seemed Timmy had been right; the coffin was manageable. Sadly, the reason was that it was just a child inside, his child.

They slowly and cautiously walked the coffin to the grave and carefully lay it on the straps.

Thankfully, the coffin was closed. Bobby knew the sight of his daughter's face would have been too much for him.

"Let us begin," the minister said.

The next fifteen minutes were essentially a blur. Bobby knew the minister was speaking but he was zoned out. His thoughts were back in Lafayette, back to happier, simpler times.

Before he knew it, the minister was tossing earth down onto the coffin. He too picked up earth and tossed it down on the coffin and, with the act, said goodbye to a third family member in the last four days.

Sasha, following her father's lead, also grabbed a handful of earth and tossed it down on the coffin as it was being lowered by the straps and a connected motor.

The minister made a final blessing and approached the family.

"Thank you. It was a nice service. Here is a donation for the church," Jerome said and handed the minister an envelope.

"I do apologize for not being able to spend much time with you but we are back up all day long, again."

Jerome looked around at all the activity in the cemetery. "I understand. Challenging times."

The minister then turned to Bobby and Sasha. "Bobby, your daughter is in a better place now."

"With our mommy," Sasha said.

The minister crouched down and took both of Sasha's hands into his.

"She is with your mommy, together, in a happy place."

Sasha hugged him

"Thank you, Minister."

The minister smiled and walked back to his cart. Bobby watched him as he did.

That was it, Bobby thought. You walk out, read a few things from what is supposed to be a holy book, shake a few hands, and walk away with an envelope full of cash.

For some reason, he was reminded of the classic Beatles' song, *Eleanor Rigby*, and specifically the line, No one was saved. From what Bobby had seen recently, no one was ever saved.

"I guess we should get back," Jerome said.

"Yeah, let's get going," Bobby replied.

They walked back to the Hummer and all climbed in.

On the way home, Sasha began to cough uncontrollably.

A Surprising Broadcast

Will was in a great mood as he packed up for his night shift. The mood was driven partially by the weight of his actions that afternoon at Costco having been lifted by the judge, but more so by the fact that Carlos wanted to change shift locations with Will.

They agreed to meet at their usual place for a couple of pre-shift drinks. Will showed up early, just before 6 pm, full of excitement.

"Will, how the hell have ya been?" the bartender asked.

"Good, of course."

"We missed you yesterday."

"Yeah, had some things to attend to."

"Well, glad you're back. The regular?"

"Yes, please."

Will settled in and looked around the bar. It looked almost deserted.

"Where is everybody?" he asked.

"Lot of folks are sick right now," the bartender replied.

Sick, sure. More like sheeple, Will thought.

His beer had just arrived when he noticed the Fox News screen on the TV behind the bar change over to an emergency broadcast.

He read the words on the screen and then muttered, "Shit."

He took his mobile phone out and opened the browser. He went to Fox online and found the same message.

"Hey, Tony, can you flip the TV to CNN?" Will asked.

"Why the fuck would I do that?"

"Cause Fox is blocked and they are saying all the channels are being blocked. I figure if CNN is blocked, then it's for real."

"Alright, alright," Tony said and grabbed the remote.

He changed the channel. It was the same message on CNN. He flipped around a few more channels. Every news channel had the same message.

"You all see this," Tony yelled out to the handful of people spread around the corners of the dark bar.

"Looks like there is a presidential speech or something at 7 pm."

"Fuck the president," Tony mumbled as he grabbed a couple of beers out of the fridge.

Carlos walked into the bar. Will turned and smiled. "Over here," he waved.

Carlos walked over and gave Will the traditional chest bump and huge bear hug.

"Hey, you gotta see this. Looks like the government is blocking all the news," Will said and they both sat at the bar.

"Shit, really? I guess that don't surprise me. I kinda figured they would do something like that," Carlos replied casually.

"We need to watch that broadcast at 7 pm," Will replied.

"Sure."

The two were joined at the bar by a couple of the backbenchers.

"What the hell is going on?" one of the regulars asked.

"I don't know. Guess we are going to find out in a bit," Carlos replied.

The next fifty minutes were interesting. Ultimately, everyone in the bar came and joined together at the bar top.

The mood wasn't good. In a state where support of the government was traditionally low, their county was decisively anti-government.

It wasn't long before the little group was calling for a revolution.

"Thank you, Will and Carlos. Thank you for being patriots and serving in our new military," one of the old-timers said.

He then stood up and saluted the two men. Everyone else in the bar stood and saluted as well.

"Hey, it's coming on," someone said.

They all took their seats and waited.

"Good evening, I speak to you from the world's capital of democracy. I also speak to you in a unique and difficult time. As I do, I am reminded of another time when America found itself at odds within her own border. At that time, President Lincoln stood, at Gettysburg, and spoke these words to our country:

We here highly resolve that these dead shall not have died in vain - that this nation, under God, shall have a new birth of freedom - and that government of the people, by the people, for the people, shall not perish from the earth.

When President Lincoln spoke these words, he too was struggling to bring the nation back together. At that time it was following a devastating civil war. As was the case then, we do not want our dead to have died in vain either. Today, we face the greatest challenge in American history since the time of the civil war. We are battling on two fronts. The first is the tiniest of enemies. A virus, that despite the fact it is invisible to the human eye, is capable of such incredible devastation. The second is the erosion of truth and with it, trust. This combination is wreaking havoc on our country and our people. As a result, I am authorizing a national state of emergency. Additionally, I am imposing a national dusk until dawn curfew. This is effective immediately. All major news media outlets have been and will continue to be shut down as will all major social media platforms. These shutdowns will remain in effect until the state of emergency is lifted.

The president took a moment to pause and gather himself.

"Additionally, the U.S. Military Forces, operating in conjunction with the National Guard is currently being deployed to manage the growing tension between red and green zones. This joint force will establish control points across all county boundaries around red zones. This action is intended to contain the virus such that it does not have the opportunity to engulf our nation. Emergency medical facilities will be established in all red zones to tend to the sick and provide vaccination services. They will also provide burial services where needed. We must respect our dead. While these actions are understandably harsh, they are required if we are to maintain the safety and stability of our nation. Updates will be provided daily at 7 pm eastern standard time. Good night and God bless."

The image on the screen faded and was replaced by a state of emergency warning.

"Jesus, it's really happening," Tony said looking up at the TV.

"You know what this means? We got our own country now," Carlos smiled.

A couple of people at the bar cheered, however not everyone seemed supportive.

"I wonder who's gonna cover my disability payments now?" one of them asked.

The bar got a little bit quieter.

"Hey, a round on the house," Tony yelled.

That brought a little cheer back.

The rest of the evening was spent debating. They discussed everything from statehood to government to budgets. Oddly, what was effectively a gift from the government— their independence—was met with less enthusiasm than one would have expected.

Another Child Falls Sick

When they arrived back at Jerome's house, they all headed to the family room and settled on the couch. Sasha was shivering so Cecilia grabbed her a blanket. Sasha curled up in it and fell asleep.

Jerome grabbed the bottle of bourbon from the kitchen and brought it back into the family room. The four adults sat themselves in the corner away from Sasha.

"Bobby, I'm worried about Sasha. The cough and the fever, it's Omega," Cecilia said.

Bobby already knew it was Omega. He had seen it, first-hand, with three members of his own family. The last thing he wanted was to see another one be taken.

"What do we do?" Bobby asked, almost in tears.

"We need a hospital, a good one, and get her help. From there, we'll get her through the vaccination process," Jerome replied.

Cecilia grabbed Bobby's hand. "You must believe in this because you will need to approve her vaccines."

"Shit, I do. I've believed for a while but I wasn't allowed to believe. So here the fuck I am, wife and one daughter gone and I'm at a cousin's with my last family and she's sick now. Yeah, fuck, I believe," Bobby replied.

"Good, good," Cecilia said as she hugged him.

"Where do we take her then?" Bobby asked.

"I made some calls today; the local hospitals are at their capacity. We could get her in possibly over the next couple of days but I think she needs help tonight," Cecilia said and stopped to ensure the message was received.

"The place to go is Altus Hospital in Baytown. We have a connection to it in our community. I can make a call now and see if we can get her in tonight," Cecilia said.

She took her mobile out and walked into the kitchen.

"How far is it?" Bobby asked.

Jerome looked at Merv for a moment. "It's about an hour and a half but we need to cross through two border zones. We're going to go from our yellow county, through a red one, then into a green one, where Baytown is. There is a wall of red counties heading north or west from here."

"Is that a problem?" Bobby asked.

"No, maybe. There are routes we can take, back ones where we can pay to get through. It's all part of a plan that the residents here put together. Call it an emergency plan. I'd have to make some other calls."

Bobby turned and looked at Jerome. A piece of him was angry—angry at the fact there were people, like Jerome, that could afford to buy an emergency plan while he was watching his family die. He also knew that the emergency plan may well save Sasha.

Cecilia walked back into the room.

"They can take Sasha tonight. We need to turn on the TV. Apparently, there is some very big breaking news," she said.

Jerome turned on his fancy new TV. He put it to Fox News, a rerun of the president's speech. It only took a few seconds for them to be glued to what they were seeing.

The speech ended; the room went quiet.

"My God, what has this come to?" Cecilia muttered.

"I think we need to leave now for Baytown," Jerome said.

"I'll get mine and Sasha's bags," Bobby said and jumped up.

"Merv, load the Hummer. I got a favor to call in," Jerome said.

"You got it."

They each headed off in their own directions. A few minutes later, they all returned to the family room. Bobby had two small bags with him, gifts from Cecilia, given they had lost just about everything with the canoe.

"I talked to our contact. They are gonna put the word out that we're coming through tonight," Jerome said.

"Go now," Cecilia said as she looked at Sasha.

Sasha was still sleeping but was visibly not well. Her skin color had changed and she was shivering.

Bobby picked up Sasha, wrapped in the blanket, and carried her out to the garage. Merv grabbed a couple of handguns and a rifle while Jerome grabbed a stack of cash from a wall safe.

Bobby settled into the back with Sasha. Jerome took the driver seat and Merv, gun in hand, took the passenger seat.

They blasted out of the garage and onto the road.

"We're going to take the 82 and then the 73. We're gonna hit a county control point on the 73. That checkpoint won't be a big deal as we'll be going from yellow to red. The bigger issue is gonna be at the back end of Chambers County and into Harris. That's where we have a quiet road and the contacts," Jerome said as he drove.

Bobby said nothing. His attention was on Sasha who had awakened and was coughing consistently.

They drove for some time in the dark. It seemed that the power was out in the area. Bobby held Sasha as they pulled up to the Jefferson County side of the checkpoint.

"Where are you folk headed?" the guard asked.

"We got a sick girl we're taking over to Baytown."

"Baytown, that's in Harris. You know it's a green zone. You gonna have some trouble there."

"Yeah, I know. We got a contact over there."

The guard looked into the Hummer and at Sasha.

"Hmmm, alright, well, good luck over there."

"Thanks."

Jerome drove on into the dark. A few minutes later, they were stopped again. It was another checkpoint, this one run by the militia inside Chambers. A small man in a poorly fitting uniform, carrying an AR-15, approached the car.

"Shit, now what?" Jerome said.

Sasha sat up. "I need to go to the bathroom," she moaned.

"Driver, get out of the car," the man screamed at Jerome.

"I think we got a problem," Jerome said, echoing the thoughts of everyone in the car.

Last Night on the Job

"We should get going," Will said as he and Carlos sat at the bar.

"Yeah, let's do one more. You need to celebrate your victory today," Carlos smiled.

There was that smile again. How could Will say no?

"Sure, let's do it," Will replied with a huge smile on his face.

Carlos ordered two more. They both chugged their beers down.

"We'll see you all tomorrow," Carlos cheered on the way out.

Carlos put his arm around Will as they walked out to Will's pickup. "Come on, little buddy, let's get to our new assignment."

They almost staggered out to the car. Both had had a little more than they should have but it was a unique night. Not just for them, but for America as a whole.

They got in the car, Carlos put the new location in the GPS, Will put on the tunes, and they hit the road.

About an hour and much singing later, they spotted their new border post. There were a lot more cars there than they were expecting.

"Look at all the cars. I'm wondering what's going on," Carlos said, concerned.

Will, seeing a moment, emboldened by alcohol, put his hand on Carlos' hand for a moment. "Hey, we'll be fine together."

Carlos turned to Will with an odd look on his face. He quickly pulled his hand back. "Hey, brother, I ain't that way, you know."

To say Will was devastated was an understatement. He had played his card, badly. The worst part was that it also put the end to hope. While never playing the card meant never truly knowing, it equally meant keeping the light of hope alive. Will, in a simple move, had just crushed his hopes.

"Of course, me either," Will stumbled to a reply.

The two awkwardly left the pickup and headed to the check-in.

"Good, you guys must be the new crew," the local lead said.

"Yeah, we transferred from the north end. Why so many people here?" Carlos replied, looking around.

"Didn't you see the news tonight? We got war."

Will looked around. While everything seemed wrong to him at that moment, bitterness was rising in him, what he saw wasn't an army preparing for war. What he saw was a bunch of out-of-shape guys who missed playing the war games they did as kids. All dressed up like tin soldiers.

He knew he was no better. Pretending to play soldier and guarding a small county road was one thing; a real war was not something Will wanted any part of. The experience with the security guard was still fresh in his mind.

"I want the two new guys manning the gate tonight, Bill and Ted, you're up top in the gatehouse, and the rest of you guys ready in the main floor bunker of the gatehouse. We need to keep a good force here in case they decide to come this way," the lead said.

"Who comes this way?" one of the crew asked.

"The goddam army."

A couple of the crew looked confused.

"Well, for anyone who missed it, our president declared war on the red zones. This is what we have been preparing for. Be ready to stand your ground tonight."

Will looked over at Carlos who had made his way to the other side of the group. Carlos avoided eye contact with him. Will's spirits dropped even further.

"Alright boys, it's duty time," the lead yelled out.

The teams all moved into position. Will and Carlos headed over to the gate.

"Looks like we got the gate together," Will said.

"Yeah, I guess we do," Carlos replied looking away.

Will also turned away. He knew he had messed up. Just as his life was getting better, once again, he tried to be the big man, and, once again, he fell flat on his face. His mother was right, he was a born loser.

Fuck Carlos, Will told himself. He didn't need anybody; he was his own man and he would prove that to everyone.

He and Carlos kept their distance as their shift passed. The night was quiet, really quiet, which just made things worse for Will. It gave him plenty of time to stew so, when a Hummer pulled up to the gate, Will was good and primed.

The Hummer pulled to a stop in front of the metal gate. Carlos held his position on the right side of the gate. Will, playing the big man, walked toward the vehicle with his AR-15 pointed directly at the driver.

"Will, we don't gotta be so hard," Carlos said.

Will looked at him with disdain.

"Driver, get out of the car," he yelled.

After a moment, the driver's door opened and a tall, black man got out.

"Yo, we just passing through. We don't want no trouble here; we're heading for Baytown. We got a sick girl with us," the driver said.

"Where are you coming from?"

"Pleasure Island, Port Arthur."

"Will, it's okay to put the gun down," Carlos yelled at him.

"Why can't you take her to a hospital there?" Will asked, gun still pointed.

"Cause there ain't no space. Look, we're coming from a yellow zone so what's the fucking problem?" the driver replied, annoyed.

"The problem is, we are the law here. We decide who comes and goes. Don't you know? It's war now."

"What the fuck are you talking about?"

The back door on the Hummer opened and someone jumped out.

Will, already hair-triggered, turned and fired. He hit the person, twice, dropping them dead in their tracks. He immediately regretted it.

Another man dropped out of the back seat of the Hummer and ran directly at Will. When the man reached Will, he bowled him over, took his gun, and began to slam the butt into Will's head against the ground. By the third hit, Will was dead.

Carlos, momentarily stunned, lifted his rifle and put a hole right through the man on top of Will. The man fell backward, dead, just like Will.

"Bobby!" Jerome screamed.

Merv, who had gotten out of the SUV to chase Sasha, turned and blew half of Carlos' face off with a 9 mm.

"Halt," came the instruction from the platform of the makeshift guardhouse.

"A little fucking late for that," Jerome screamed at them.

Merv dropped his gun and picked up Sasha's body. He carried it into the light for everyone to see

"What the fuck are you people doing? What is wrong with you? You're pathetic little tin soldiers, playing God. Look what you made today, you fucking assholes. We're just people, trying to survive, and you killed us," Jerome screamed.

No one responded. They were just tin soldiers, they all knew that at that point. They playing at a game that was far beyond them. Silence was the best answer any of them could give at that point.

Jerome and Merv carried Sasha's body and placed it in the back of the Hummer. They then did the same with Bobby's body.

They walked to the front of the Hummer, preparing to get in when something down the road caught their attention.

"What the hell is that?" Merv asked.

The Church of the Plague

Jimmy, Big Al, and DeSantos followed a couple of guys dragging what was a very sick Mickey. Worse, of all, they were all following a crazy woman.

"DeSantos, do you know which church we are heading to?" Big Al asked.

"Honestly, I dunno. I haven't done much work with her. I always dealt with her son. This woman is nuts. I didn't know."

"Now we're stuck following her to who knows where," Jimmy said.

"Well, it's a church, so it can't be that bad," DeSantos said.

After trudging along for some fifteen minutes, they came upon a small, wooded area just off the country road they had been following. They turn up a small dirt road.

A couple of minutes later, they came upon a church. Taren raised her hands to the sky and said, "Praise the Lord."

She turned back and looked at them all with a crazed look in her eyes.

"Jesus," Big Al muttered.

They were quickly approaching the church when Jimmy stopped dead.

"I've seen this place," he said, trembling.

"What, you been here before?" DeSantos asked.

"No, I've seen it, in a dream."

"I've seen it too, except it was more like a nightmare," Big Al replied.

"I ain't going inside," Jimmy said.

"Shit, man, I don't think the crazy lady is gonna like that," DeSantos said.

"I don't wanna go in either," Big Al said.

"Alright. We wait here. We'll wait for whatever they're gonna do for sick boy."

The three guys sat down in the grass, intending to wait.

A couple of minutes later, several large men walked out of the church carrying shotguns. Taren stepped out in front of them.

"DeSantos and the rest of ya, we need you to join us," she yelled.

"Shit, I guess we're going in," DeSantos said.

"Fuck," Jimmy said and stood up.

He looked closely at the church. The church was a typical northeastern rural model. The outside was quite run down, as it was in Jimmy's dream.

While it was quite typical looking from the outside; the inside was quite a different story. Most of the traditional pews were gone, replaced with a series of tents and cots. There was a smell of gasoline. The lights were on and Jimmy quickly figured the gasoline was for a generator he could hear pumping away outside.

A priest stood on the altar in traditional flowing garb. The gown held patches of red on the holy white. The man turned and looked at Jimmy and the crew.

"I am Father Ken Godevenos. This is my church, The Church of the Plague," he shouted and began to laugh.

Just a Shame

Darkness hung in the air. No one moved inside the guardhouse. No one, it seemed, wanted to involve themselves in the tragic scene that lay before them.

Jerome and Merv stood beside the Hummer, preparing to leave.

A tall man, odd in demeanor, all dressed in gray, casually walked down the street and into the scene. He whistled a tune as he did. Jerome quickly recognized it, it was '*When the Saints go Marching in*'.

The man walked right up to the bodies of Will and Carlos, and looked down onto them. He stopped whistling and the air went still. He slowly did a 360, carefully looking at everyone as he did.

"What we have here is a failure to communicate," he said in a thick southern accent. Again, no one said a word.

The gray man then looked directly at Jerome. "It's a shame, you know, this whole thing," he said.

Jerome nodded. "I know."

The gray man nodded back. He turned and walked casually back, the same way he had walked in.

Jerome and Merv climbed back into the Hummer. He looked at Merv and said, "Let's go home."

The Omega Variant

The Blood of the Innocent

Mickey was dragged up onto the altar while Jimmy and the others were forced to sit in a row of pews that still stood next to the altar. Two men, holding shotguns, stood watch over them.

Taren placed herself on a side of the altar where she kneeled and prayed.

"What the fuck?" Big Al whispered to Jimmy.

'What the fuck' was probably the exact description Jimmy would give at that moment as well.

Jimmy and crew, as well as dozens of others, all sat and watched as Mickey was laid out on a table.

Jimmy had flashed back to his dream at that moment. He knew what was coming next.

"Holy shit, I can't tell you why I know this but something really bad is about to happen to a child," he whispered to Big Al.

The church doors burst open again and a child was carried across the room by two large, strong men. One of the men, who had a real nasty look to him, kept his large, grimy hand tightly clasped over the child's mouth.

The child, a boy, was perhaps ten or eleven. He was terrified. He was struggling as best he could but was no match for the men who held him. Whether or not he knew what was in store for him, Jimmy didn't know, but he fought as though he did.

The boy was brought up onto the altar and laid across the baptismal basin.

"Shit, it's really happening. They're going to slit the boy's throat," Jimmy said.

Just as Jimmy finished speaking, the priest pulled out a straight razor and slit the boy's throat. The incision was deep and the blood poured out freely. While most of it accumulated in the basin, it also splashed along the floor and onto the priest himself.

As the blood spilled, Taren became like a rabid dog. She was howling for blood. Many others in the church pushed their way to the altar, also screaming for the blood.

The child's body was tossed aside, into a corner.

"Bring me the sick," Father Godevenos said.

Two men brought Mickey over to the priest.

"Big Al, you smoke, right?" Jimmy asked quietly.

"Yeah, why?"

"You got a lighter on you?"

"Yeah."

"I got a plan. I saw some gas cans at the back of the altar. When everyone gets up on the altar to drink the blood, we rush up there too, knock over a couple of the gas cans, and you toss the lighter in."

"You sure they are all going to jump up onto the altar?"

"Yeah, I'm sure."

"Hey, you two, no talking," a man holding a shotgun yelled at them.

The priest put a small cup into the blood and slowly let it drip down into Mickey's throat.

The priest stopped, dipped the cup in the blood again, and drank it down.

"Come, come get your cure," he screamed.

Taren rushed to the basin and scooped out blood with her hands, and drank it down. The rest of the congregation quickly made their way up onto the altar, equally craving the boys' blood.

"Now," Jimmy yelled.

He and Big Al jumped up onto the altar and joined the congregation moving towards the basin. DeSantos quickly picked up on what they were doing and jumped into the group as well.

The shotgun-wielding guys jumped up as well. "Hey, sit down," one of them yelled.

Jimmy knew there was no way they would be able to shoot at them if they were mixed in with everyone else, especially not with a shotgun.

The three of them headed directly for the rear of the altar. When they got there, Jimmy quickly pulled the cap off one of the gas cans and tossed it onto the altar floor near the basin. Gas began to cover the floor.

The congregation barely noticed the gas as they blindly pushed forward toward the blood basin.

Jimmy looked at Big Al, who, on cue, took out an old-school lighter, lit it, and tossed it into the gas. Fire immediately ignited and quickly caught everyone on the altar.

Jimmy smiled at Taren as she turned and looked at him with fire climbing up her. Her reaction stunned him. He expected her to scream or cry, something in that vein. Instead, she grinned at him, a horrifying grin, and turned back to the basin and put her hands right back into the blood.

"We gotta get out of here," Jimmy stammered.

The two men with shotguns were pushing their way toward Jimmy and the other two. Jimmy realized they were trapped at the back of the altar by fire and guns.

DeSantos turned and leaped through a stained-glass window, falling on the lawn behind the church.

"Fuck it," Jimmy said and jumped out the window. Big Al quickly followed.

The three guys got up and looked back at the church. The flames were quickly growing.

"Come on, follow me," DeSantos said.

The three men ran like bats out of hell into the closest wooded area. There, they stopped to catch their breath.

Jimmy chanced a moment to look back at the church. Something was driving him to look. The scene brought him back to his dream. Light was emanating from church. He assumed the light was from the growing fire, as it was in the dream, however, something was off; the color wasn't right, not for a fire of that nature. It was too white. He turned away.

"Guys, we need to get to the ferry pick-up point tonight as planned. We don't show and there ain't no second chance," DeSantos said.

"How far is it?" Jimmy asked.

"From here, about six miles, I'm guessing."

"You know the way?"

"Once we find a main road, I will."

"How much time do we have?"

DeSantos looked down at his watch. "About three hours."

"Then we better get going."

All Good Things Must Come to an End

A man, all dressed in gray, strolled into the president's office. The president looked up from his desk. "Who are you? How did you get in here?" the president asked, concerned.

"Who am I?" the gray man laughed.

The president looked toward the door. The gray man turned, looked at the door, and then back to the president. "There is no salvation awaiting you out there."

He continued to walk until he reached the president's desk. "May I?" he asked politely.

The president waved his arm at one of the chairs. "Please, be my guest."

The gray man sat down in the chair. "As to how I got in here, well, I believe you invited me."

The president glanced again at the door. It slammed shut. He looked back at the gray man.

"Do you really want to know who I am?" the gray man asked. As he did, the room drew completely black.

The president put his pen down. "I know who you are," he said.

The gray man clapped his hands a couple of times, laughing. "Bravo, bravo." The room brightened again.

Music started to play in the room. It was the Rolling Stones' *Sympathy for the Devil*. The gray man smiled and then sang, "Please allow me to introduce myself. I'm a man of wealth and taste. I've been around for a long, long year. Stole million man's souls an faith."

He stopped singing and the music stopped.

He leaned forward and stared at the president with pitch-black eyes. "So, here we are, you and I. You, the last President of the United States of America and me, well, I rode a tank, held a general's rank when the blitzkrieg raged and the bodies stank," he laughed.

He then became serious. "You know, the bodies stank then and they stink now."

The president did everything he could to steady himself. "I don't disagree with you. What do you want?"

The gray man stood up and looked around the room. He took his time and wandered over to the portraits of past presidents.

"Well, the end, of course. Every song, every story, has an end. This virus, it is humanity's end."

The gray man walked back around the desk and sat down again.

"Have we no say in the matter?"

"You've had a say for a long time. On top of that, you've had tips all along the way. Let's take all the bullshit about God and religion away. The fact is, what was given to you in the form of the Bible, the Quran, and all the other sources of 'advice' were intended to be guides, ones to help you evolve. Humanity turned them into weapons."

"In our defense, if I'm permitted, the information was provided to a very immature species at the time," the president replied.

The gray man looked closely at the president. "True, but it was at a critical point of your evolution. Sink or swim, you might call it. You were evolving, intellectually, and it was clear that you would reach a point where you would develop great power. The nature of power that could be disruptive to the fabric of the universe around you. You need to be tested. We needed to know if you could be trusted."

"And this virus, it is the last test I take it?"

"Call it an opportunity for humanity to band together and work as a species. Yes, the last one."

The president stood up. He steadied himself as anger was starting to rise in him.

"It sounds to me as though you created a deadly virus to do more than test us."

The gray man grinned. It seemed that he enjoyed the challenge.

"I, we, don't create anything. We observe and communicate, when and where we believe it to be appropriate. Nature created this as it does periodically, part of its self-cleansing process you could say. We knew it was coming and we knew it would come in waves. Each wave gave you the opportunity to learn, adjust and evolve. The waves played out in such a manner that gave humanity many opportunities to right yourselves. You didn't."

"So, is there no hope?" the president asked, sitting back down again, the steam in him gone.

"The test, or the virus if you prefer, was your hope. It knows no borders. It didn't stop moving because there was a line on your map. It forced you to recognize the limitations in the structure of your world. You have not even been able to work together as a country, let alone a world. Do you believe there is any hope?"

The president said nothing. He thought back to the meetings that he had had with the supposedly bipartisan group. The gray man was right. They couldn't, even in the face of impending doom, find enough common ground.

The gray man stood up and walked to the window. He looked out over the lawn.

"The funny thing is, your Bible, for what it's worth, talks about humans being thrown out of the Garden of Eden. What you don't realize is your world is a heaven, within the greater universe. What do you do with this heaven? You've been slowly destroying it."

The gray man turned and smiled. "Not to worry, it will return to the heaven it was for the remaining life on earth. Did you not wonder why the virus does not kill any species other than you? In time, another civilization will rise here."

The president thought about what the gray man had just said. It seemed the truth was, nature decided. Nature was saving the rest of heaven from the plague that was humanity.

"Why tell me this? Why not tell the world?" the president asked.

"You don't mind if I smoke, do you?" the gray man asked as he returned to his seat.

The president looked at him with surprise. "No, please, enjoy," he replied.

The gray man pulled a cigar out of his vest pocket. "Cuban," he said, smiling.

He lit the cigar.

"Not unlike humanity's misinterpretation of the Bible, your interpretation of me, or us, is also off the mark. I am not evil in the manner I am described. For clarity, I am not an 'I'. I am far greater than a single entity, but you are unable to understand these concepts at your stage of evolution."

He pulled in a long drag of his cigar. He blew the smoke out. The smoke formed a complex image. It appeared to be the Earth surrounded by wispy forms. The view of the image pulled back and what appeared was a complex image of the universe. The image was incredibly detailed and almost felt alive. The gray man waved his hand and the scene disappeared.

"This world is just part of a greater, universal ecosystem. All things, matter, and souls are tested periodically. Think of what has happened as the almighty survival-of-the-fittest test. Unfortunately, humanity failed," he said and pulled another drag of his cigar.

"To your question, I am telling every major leader in your world at this exact moment."

"So, how does this end?" the president asked.

"Through a natural process. I, we, do not provide information on the future. Doing so would influence your free will, which is a fundamental underpinning of this universe."

"How long do we have?"

"Again, I cannot provide you specifics. It will depend on humanity's behavior, which I remind you is what brought us to this point."

The president nodded. He knew the time for debate had passed.

The gray man stood and reached his hand across the oval desk. The president stood and knowingly shook hands, not just with the gray man, but with the universal structure he represented.

"Thank you, Mr. President. For what it is worth, I do regret this falling on your duty. There were many presidents who were far below you in capability. There are many realities of this universe. Unfortunately for you, one of them is timing."

The gray man bowed, turned, and quietly walked back out the door.

A Ferry from Heaven

The three men quickly found a road that DeSantos recognized. From there, it was just a matter of following memory.

"Hey, what the hell happened back there?" Big Al asked as they walked.

"What do you mean?" DeSantos asked.

"What do I mean? That whole fucked up situation. They killed a kid and drank his blood. Then there is that bloody nut job, Taren."

"Ah, that was some messed-up shit."

"You should have seen the look she gave me after we set that fire," Jimmy said.

"Pissed, I bet," DeSantos replied.

"No, she grinned at me."

"Shit, that was one messed-up woman," Big Al said.

"It's one messed-up world," Jimmy replied.

"Hey, are we gonna have any issues with the ferry without Phil?"

"Na, he just set up the connection. I manage it now."

"So, this your last trip?" Jimmy asked.

"Yeah. I used to charge two grand a head for this escape but there ain't no money no more. $500 a head just covers my costs. I figure it's time to get out."

That ended the conversation. They walked on in silence.

A couple of hours later, they arrived at Lake Ontario. The three sat down and took a moment to look out across the water.

"That's Canada over there?" Big Al asked.

"Yup," DeSantos replied, taking a joint out.

"What time you got?" Big Al asked.

"2:30 am. We got about thirty minutes, but we need to make our way west a little. We're at the top of Norway Road. We got almost a mile or so to get to Bald Eagle Creek. There is a small port there and that's where our boat will be."

Jimmy stood up. "Well, let's get going. I ain't missing this ride."

The three men, although exhausted, got up and covered the last stretch. They were so close to freedom they could smell it. Jimmy worried that perhaps it was just a tease, that something was still to go wrong. It would be consistent with how his life had played out.

However, this time, nothing went wrong and they arrived with about ten minutes to spare. They hunkered down in the long grass across from a marina.

"Alright, boys. We sit and wait now," DeSantos said.

That was exactly what they did. They each grabbed a spot, close enough to remain a group, but far enough to disconnect, mentally, from each other. No one wanted to talk anymore.

Jimmy sat up high on the grass, on a spot that allowed him a view across the lake, at Canada. He could see lights, lots of them. The power was on there, or so it seemed.

His thoughts went back to his sister. He had never gotten back to her about the funeral. Why would he? He had nothing but more crap to tell her. The same crap he had been telling everyone his whole life, how he was going to change, be a better person.

No, she was best being spared the last lie. He wondered for a moment if she was even still alive.

A light flashed across the bay. "That's our ride, boys."

The three of them scurried down the grassy hillside to the waterfront. An old ferry sat about thirty yards out in the bay.

Jimmy and Big Al looked at DeSantos. "Well, you want freedom, jump in," DeSantos said.

DeSantos jumped in the water and swam to the ferry. Jimmy looked at Big Al and they both jumped in.

"Holy shit, this is cold," Big Al yelled out.

Ten minutes later, all three of them were sitting below deck, wrapped in blankets, drinking a good whiskey.

Big Al held his glass up. "To freedom."

They all clinked glasses.

"DeSantos, I'm sorry, I gotta ask, who was the girl?" Jimmy asked.

DeSantos laughed. "Funny, you know, I really thought one of ya would have asked that question long before this. She's the cousin of my buddy that used to run that safe house. I made a promise I would get her back there if something happened to him."

"You got her there and left her," Big Al said.

"We all left something behind," Jimmy muttered.

The three sat drinking their whiskey, quietly preparing for a new life.

A young man clambered down the ferry's stairs. "We're approaching the shore."

DeSantos stood up. "Well, guys, this is where we part ways."

"What do you mean?" Jimmy asked concerned.

"Look, I'm sorry. We can't be connected if you guys get caught, so, you guys are gonna swim ashore here."

Jimmy jumped up and grabbed DeSantos by the throat. "Are you fucking us? If you are, I'll kill you."

DeSantos casually slid Jimmy's hand from his throat. "I'm not fucking you. If I wanted to fuck you, I would have done it in the tunnels in New York."

Jimmy stepped back. He knew DeSantos was right.

"So, how far we gotta swim?"

"About 100 yards. You'll have waterproof backpacks with fresh clothes."

Jimmy looked back at Big Al and turned to DeSantos. He put his hand out. DeSantos clasped his hand and hugged him.

"Shit, man, I'm sorry, brother. Thanks for everything. We're here, we're free," Jimmy said, almost teary.

"You and Big Al get your asses out of here. Good luck, we all need it in this world."

The man who had come down the stairs led them back up. When they reached the deck, they were each given a little backpack.

"That's the eastern coast side of the Toronto area. Once you get inland, find the authorities and declare yourselves as refugees. They'll take you in," the man said.

Big Al looked at Jimmy. "You ready?"

"Fuck yeah."

The two leaped off the back of the ferry with smiles on their faces.

The Final Act

The President stood and looked out the window of the Oval Office once again. While the scene looked as it always had, he knew the America behind it, was no longer what it was.

There was a knock on the door.

"Come in," the President said.

Jim walked into the room and headed over to the window beside the President.

"It's time, Sir. We have the military debrief."

"What can I expect?"

"Nothing good, Sir. The situation on the southern front continues to degrade. Our forces are facing increased defection to the local militias. The militias have made inroads into several major green regions."

The President looked at Jim for a moment and then back out the window.

"Thank you, Jim. Give me a minute and I'll meet you in the briefing room."

Jim nodded and turned to leave. He then stopped and looked back at the president.

"Oh, Sir, there is one other thing."

"Yes, Jim?"

"There is another variant."

"Yes, I know, Jim."

The Last Variant

For the first time since his childhood, Jimmy felt at home. Canada, as it turned out, was the dream it had been made out to be.

He was still in quarantine, in one of many quarantine locations that the Toronto region had allocated to refugees. He had another five weeks to go in there. It was a standard process for anyone who wanted to enter Canada. The individual entering the country accepted the quarantine and the associated vaccine process or they were not provided entry, ever.

The interesting thing was that nearly 99% of those who managed to reach the border accepted the conditions, and found themselves a better place.

The quarantine location was the last step in the refugee process. Jimmy had already gone through a criminal background check, a full medical, and two shots of the new Candian three-shot cycle to gain immunity.

He lay on one of the couches in the shared living area, occasionally looking up at the TV. Big Al was seated up by the TV with a couple of other guys who had also managed to sneak across Lake Ontario.

Big Al had been tied to the news since they arrived. It was a Canadian government-run station as all the American media networks were being blocked. The big story was the civil war raging across parts of America, particularly in the south.

"Hey, looks like the Texas free state militia took Dallas overnight. They got the whole state now except for some areas in Houston," Big Al yelled over to Jimmy.

Big Al liked to keep Jimmy in the loop on the state of affairs back in America. It seemed the worse things got, the happier Big Al was. Lafayette and the rest of Louisiana had fallen to local militia groups right after the big announcement. It seemed the challenge now was getting the various militias to work together. In some ways, it seemed no different to Jimmy than the situation in Afghanistan between the warlords when the U.S. had invaded. For Jimmy, all militias were essentially the same.

"That's great, Big Al."

A breaking news report popped up on the screen. It was from the World Health Organization. Jimmy lifted his head to watch it.

"Breaking news out of the WHO. A new variant, yet unnamed, has now been detected in Africa, America, and Europe. This variant, at present, seems to evade the recent vaccines, including the support booster. Additionally, it appears to have a mortality rate approaching 60%," the news anchor.

The room, which had been its usual boisterous self, fell silent.

Jimmy lay his head back down and did something he had never done in his life. He prayed.

The End

Other Works by Sean O'Neil

Romantic and Adventure Thrillers

Brian's Stolen Dream
Sahara's Miracle
Parminder's Legacy
James's Game
Love in a Time of EMPs

The Supernatural Thriller Series

The Comatose Diaries
Grindhouse Canada, Urban Legends from the Great White North
Grindhouse Caribbean, Urban Legends from across the Islands
The Chosen
The Omega Variant

The Apocalyptic Series

The Plague, Judgement Day
Demons, Judgement Day

YA Fantasy

The Chinese Door (with David Tsubouchi)

Manufactured by Amazon.ca
Bolton, ON

24477859R00155